Pinch
River

Other books by Helen Godfrey Pyke

Cancer at 3:00 A. M.
Doctor, Doctor
The Heart Remembers
No Peace for a Soldier
Any Sacrifice but Conscience
Why Can't I Do School?

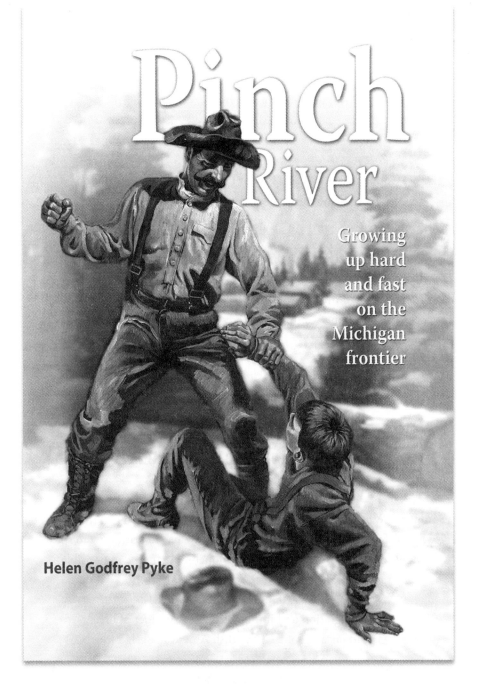

Pinch River

Growing
up hard
and fast
on the
Michigan
frontier

Helen Godfrey Pyke

Pacific Press® Publishing Association
Nampa, Idaho
Oshawa, Ontario, Canada
www.pacificpress.com

Cover design by Gerald Lee Monks
Cover design resources by Marcus Mashburn
Inside design by Steve Lanto

Additional copies of this book are available by calling toll-free 1-800-765-6955
or online at http://www.adventistbookcenter.com.

Library of Congress Cataloging-in-Publication Data

Pyke, Helen Godfrey.
Pinch River : growing up hard and fast on the Michigan frontier /
Helen Godfrey Pyke.
p. cm.
Summary: When twelve year old Sven immigrates to Michigan from Sweden
with his father, to work in a logging camp, he has to learn how to speak
English, stay out of trouble, endure loneliness, and be responsible.
ISBN-13: 978-0-8163-2250-3 (pbk.)
ISBN-10: 0-8163-2250-3 (pbk.)
[1. Emigration and immigration. 2. Conduct of life.
3. Fathers and sons. 4. Swedish Americans.] I. Title.

PZ7.P9877Pi 2008
dc22

2007038781

08 09 10 11 12 • 5 4 3 2 1

Dedication

To my grandson Niki,

whose interest in the unfolding story

encouraged me as I wrote it.

Contents

From Stockholm to South Bend

"Two years is a long time," Sven Anderson said. "Lesja will be as tall as I am now, and Karen will be—Mama will need—" He couldn't finish. His throat felt as if he'd swallowed a chunk of dry bread that wouldn't go down. The gangplank of the great steamship *Belking* had been drawn in. Though he thought he could still see Mama and his sisters and infant brother in the crowd on the pier, with his eyes swimming in tears, he wasn't certain.

Papa's hand was firm on his shoulder. "Two years? Hardly any time at all, son. Two years ago you were ten years old just like Lesja is now. And overnight you have sprung up from a child to a young man almost as tall as your papa. I'm sorry we have to part like this. But Mama and the children can stay with Grandfather Oldstrom with no cost to us. In two years we two can earn a good bit and find a farm. We'll build a house, so when Mama comes, she'll have a home instead of room in a tenement like we've lived in since Uncle Jens put us off the homestead."

The ship's engines surged, and the deck shuddered. The liner began to move away from the dock. Sven did not brush away the tears. A stiff Baltic breeze coming into Stockholm harbor dried them as they clung to his lashes. He wondered if Papa was right.

Sven wanted to sit down on his bundle of clothing tied with rope and cry as Lesja would have. Instead, he stood with the bundle wedged between his ankles and his knees. Nothing must separate him from the bundle, for in it were his few garments and the treasures he had taken from the old home when they moved to the city. Papa carried a bundle too. But his money was sewn into a second pocket on the inside of his trousers, one with no opening to the outside.

A year ago, Sven would have argued with anyone who suggested Papa was not always right. But since Uncle Jens came back from the war and pushed them off the farmstead that had belonged to the family for probably ten generations, Sven could see there were some things over which Papa had no control and some situations that Papa did not fully understand. It was nice to be growing up so quickly, nice to be almost as tall as Papa. But it was terribly scary to know that everything wouldn't turn out fine just because Papa said it would.

Papa's fingers relaxed their grip on Sven's shoulder, and his hand fell to his side. Sven looked at him and saw tears like a row of small crystals quivering on his lower lashes.

*   *   *   *   *

The ship *Belking* left the dock at half past noon. Like most of the other emigrants, Sven and Papa stood on deck watching until the Swedish shoreline melted into a gray line along the northeastern horizon and then disappeared. Finally, the crowd melted too, flowing down the hatches to quarters below.

"Twenty-three hundred passengers," Papa said, as if he didn't believe the number.

"It's a huge boat," Sven agreed.

"We're packed like pickled herring in a barrel," Papa said. "You and I will share a bunk. If it's wide enough, we might both fit on it if we sleep on our sides."

Sven laughed. "At least we won't be so lonesome." He picked up his bundle and followed Papa below.

"Meals come with our passage," Papa said. "When the call goes up, I'll go first while you stay with our belongings. I'll hurry back in time for you to get in line. I can tell you how it's done once I've been to the dining room."

Indeed, Papa had waited so long for his place at the table in the vast dining room that Sven hardly had to wait at all. He sat with his white enameled bowl and wolfed down the thick potato-and-fish stew. Then he quickly left, for still other passengers were waiting to eat.

* * * * *

The following morning the ship passed out of the Baltic Sea into the North Sea. When they bought passage, Papa had shown Sven on the map the route they would be taking. Sven knew they would come into Baltimore harbor in America and that they would take a train to Chicago, a city hundreds of miles west of the American Atlantic coast. North of Chicago they would work in the pine forests as loggers.

"Michigan," he said, testing the word.

Sven was worried about a lot of things besides missing Mama and the younger children. He had never even heard a person speak English, and yet in America everyone would be speaking English. On the farm he had always split the firewood for their home, but Papa had always sawed it. If things worked out the way Papa said they would, he'd be spending most of his time limbing trees with an ax. He wasn't even sure that, after living two years in the cramped city tenement, he still remembered how to swing an ax.

"You'll like working in the forests," Papa said. "When I was a young man, your grandfather sent me to the mountains to cut timber. The pine resins smell so fresh. The winds blow through the boughs at night like angel music while you sleep."

"Will there be mountains?" Sven asked.

"Pine forests generally grow in the mountains," Papa said. "You'll enjoy the mountains."

Until we leave the ship, Sven thought, *nearly everyone will speak Swedish.* That gave him some comfort.

Papa was not a man given to much talk. Yet during the long hours on the ship, he listened a great deal to other Swedes talking about their plans. Many of the men were like him, displaced from a life of farming and going to America to buy farms. Some had failed at business and hoped to do better with a fresh start in the "land of promise." Some young men came from crowded cities where they had found few opportunities.

"See, Sven," Papa said as they lay in their bunk one night. "It is for you as much as for me that we have left Sweden. What could you hope for? Hard work with low pay. You would never own an acre of land. And always you would be at the mercy of people with land and money."

The next day Sven watched a group of men milling on the deck. They were a loud and hopeful crowd, though hardly old enough to grow beards. If he were twenty, he might feel as hopeful as they.

Papa learned that logging in Michigan began after the first autumn snowfall and lasted through March, possibly into April, when the snow melted from the forests. Then experienced and very skilled loggers might hire on as "river pigs," driving logs down the rivers to the mills. Most lumberjacks worked on southern Michigan farms through the summer. After the harvest they would buy clothing and gear for the next winter and then go back to the pineries.

"We're lucky I heard this now," Papa said. "We came at a disadvantage with no letters from relatives to tell us what to expect and how to find good work. Oats have been cut now, but we should find farmers who need help with the wheat harvest."

"It's work, you know," Sven said. "And I can bind sheaves or carry."

"We're going to need wages," said Papa. "My money won't last forever."

* * * * *

The Atlantic passage was swift but rough. The *Belking* sliced through the waves; and Sven, standing sometimes with Papa on deck, watched the dark smoke from her smokestacks float swiftly away behind them. He did not grow sick as many of the passengers did, but he did not feel well either when the ship plunged through twenty-foot waves, and emigrants who tried to walk the decks were thrown against each other and nearly overboard. On the eleventh day, they awoke in the calm water of Baltimore harbor. A train connected almost from the dock, and after going through customs, Papa bought tickets for Chicago.

Sven climbed into the rail carriage with Papa, and like Papa, swinging his bundle of possessions. Papa found them a bench, and they set their bundles between their feet as they sat down. All the rail passengers had been on their vessel or another lying at the next dock over. Around him Sven still heard the familiar sounds of Swedish, and an old woman was crooning a Swedish lullaby to a little girl in her lap.

The rail carriage was twice as long as a farm wagon. It was attached to other carriages front and back, that were also hitched to other carriages. Finally, they hitched a locomotive at the head of the train and at the rear a short carriage with only two trainmen inside. Sven fingered the leather strap that held the rolled side curtain above the open window. He ran his hand down the post. The whistle sounded. A trainman shouted, and they began to move so slowly that Sven thought at first the station had taken to wheels and was moving away. Then the carriage shook and jerked, and the carriage behind jerked, and the jerk traveled down the row of carriages until they all rolled down the track, gaining speed.

The tracks led between tenements, newer than where his family had lived in Stockholm, but taller and even darker. He saw children leaning out of windows and shirts and petticoats flying like banners from clotheslines high above the tracks. Ash and tiny cinders floated down from the cloud of coal smoke trailing the locomotive, settling on the not-very-clean clothes. The train came out then into woodland, and then small farms pressed against the tracks. Horses grazed nearby, and the cows hardly lifted their heads from the flat meadows to look at the train.

The train stopped at towns, but Papa and Sven stayed in their seats. "If we move, we might not have a seat to come back to," Papa warned.

Sven wondered about meals. *Will a trainman come with bread and meat?*

The tracks followed a river into hills. Before dusk Sven saw mountains rising in the sunset. The train swayed on the curves as the railroad grade followed the curves of the river and rose up the valley. In the darkness, Sven tried to see the shape of the land. Though the train lurched and shuddered, stopping and starting throughout the night, Sven slept on the hard bench, slumped against Papa. In his dreams the train's whistle echoed through Mama's song as she plaited Lesja's golden hair, as she held his tiny brother to her breast, as she rested her arm around his own shoulders, pressing her soft cheek to his, as she took rye bread from the oven. In his dreams Mama broke off a chunk of bread for him, and the warm aroma filled his nose. But even in his sleep, the bread did not touch his lips.

He awoke in early dawn so hungry he could think of nothing else. He would welcome a ship's hard biscuit and the fish-and-potato stew he had grown tired of.

They were passing through mountains. But these mountains were not covered with pine forests or larch or linden. They were dark green with oaks and other trees Sven did not recognize, even when the branches almost brushed the sides of the train. The tracks still curved with the curve of the river, but now they were descending. Sometime in the night they had crossed into a different watershed.

The train stopped twice at towns before Papa mentioned food.

Other passengers got off and came back with loaves of bread and blocks of cheese. One woman bought apples for her children.

Papa rose when the whistle blew and the train slowed for the next town. He set his bundle on the seat. "I'll buy bread."

Sven guessed Papa's money must be almost gone, for he bought nothing else. Papa broke off a small piece and ate it slowly. Sven took an even smaller piece, measuring the length of the loaf against two more days' travel.

Toward evening they dropped out of the closed valleys into a broad one where the river meandered through meadows. The train took a direct course toward a large town. Here the woman and her several children, passengers who had come off their ship in Baltimore, got off. Their seats were taken by six businessmen in black suits and white collars, all speaking rapidly in English. Other passengers came back with pastries. A woman handed Sven a small pie, no bigger than a walnut.

"Thanks," he said.

Its crust was fragile as crumbling sand. Inside it was filled with bright-yellow preserves.

Papa ate a small chunk of bread from their loaf as the carriage grew dark. He nodded to Sven but did not offer him a portion. Sven knew the little pie had been his supper.

At daybreak the train took them through low hills and shallow valleys. It stopped at a city where the businessmen prepared to leave. One of the men handed Sven the curved remnant of a sausage.

"Thanks," Sven said.

When they were gone, he took a deep bite and handed the remainder to Papa. That was their breakfast. Papa did not bring out the shrinking loaf of bread.

The next day Sven awoke in land so absolutely flat it might have been a table and all the houses and trees and animals only toys arranged by children to amuse themselves. He wanted to speak to someone, but Papa was more silent than usual, and all around them were people who spoke only English among themselves. In late afternoon Papa grew agitated. He got off the train at nearly every stop and came back to sit nervously on the wooden bench.

Finally he said, "One more stop, Sven. We get off before Chicago, for we will work in Michigan. They're hiring loggers in South Bend,

Indiana. We'll sign up with a logging company and learn the particulars about getting north in October. Then we'll cast about for field work here."

*   *   *   *   *

In the station Sven grasped the rope that tied his bundle and rested one foot on Papa's bundle. Around him swarmed thirty or more men and boys, all speaking Swedish. The men drifted away in the direction Papa had gone, and the boys stayed in the vaulted waiting room. A boy a bit taller and a great deal thinner than Sven flipped his head to throw back his hair from his forehead. He grinned.

"Hello," he said. "It's been a long train ride." He wasn't speaking Swedish, but something similar.

"Hello," Sven said. "Are you hiring on as a logger in Michigan?"

"My father and me and my brother," the boy said. "My uncle is already there. We're going up to work with him. I'm Carl Helgesen. That's my brother, Bernard, looking out the window."

Sven held out his hand. "I'm Sven Anderson. Are you a Norske?"

Carl grinned. "Sure I am."

"Did you leave your mother and the others in Norway?"

Carl's eyes clouded. "That we did. Mama died last winter. Aunt Marji took the little ones to keep. We won't be going back, and they'll not come here to join us. I guess we'll never see them again."

"I'm sorry," Sven said.

"Life's that way," Carl said. "We do the best we can. My father says we've a chance to make good here. The three of us are strong and able. Uncle can help us make a start. He's a superintendent, building up a new camp. He's got work for us right away." Carl nodded toward the far end of the room. "Is that your father coming back now? He looks like he's pleased about how things worked out for him."

"Carl, I hope we end up working for the same company," Sven said.

"That's not likely. Michigan is a big place, and lots of logging companies are taking out the timber."

"I wish you well," Sven said.

Carl grinned and tossed his hair back, but Sven guessed that he, too, was uncertain about what lay ahead.

*   *   *   *   *

"I signed on for McEllroy Logging Company," Papa said. "Here's our pass north." He held up two railroad tickets. "And there's a farmers' market down the street where we can look for work. If we can get on, we'll have bed and meals until we finish, and then cash pay."

They shouldered their bundles and headed down the street.

The market, they found, was a place where country people brought produce from gardens and fields to sell to townsfolk. Wagons lined the square under the shade of towering elms. The wagons were loaded with apples, potatoes, cabbages, and large round fruits with puckered tan skin, and even larger ones with skin a shiny green with darker green stripes.

Papa nudged Sven. "Hungry?"

"Don't spend your money until you find us jobs," Sven said. "I can wait."

Papa picked up a tan fruit and sniffed it. He held it to Sven's nose. The smell was strange but wonderfully musky and rich.

"How much?" Papa asked the woman sitting on the wagon tailgate.

She shook her head. "English."

Papa fished in his pocket and brought out a few coins and held them in the palm of his hand. "How much?" he asked again in Swedish.

The woman took up a thin silver coin. She nodded to Papa, satisfied.

"Was that a good price?" Sven asked.

"I don't think so," Papa said. "A logger works for a dollar a day. Ten dimes make a dollar. What do you think?"

"I hope it tastes good."

They moved down the square to a wagon that had been filled with potatoes but was now nearly empty. The farmer had brought his team and was preparing to hitch the horses to the wagon. His son scooped the last potatoes into burlap bags for a grocer, whose small cart stood ready.

Papa approached the farmer. "Do you need potato pickers?" he asked.

The farmer looked him up and down. "Norske?"

"Swede," Papa said. He handed the large fruit to Sven and mimed picking up potatoes from the ground.

"Sure," the farmer said. He held up two fingers, then pointed to Sven and Papa.

"Two of us," Papa said.

"The name's Schmidt," the farmer said.

"Anderson," Papa replied.

Mr. Schmidt motioned for them to climb into the wagon. Papa nodded vigorously but held up his hand. He took the fruit to the refuse pile and sliced it open. He scooped out the seeds and pocketed his knife. Sven climbed into the wagon, and Papa came behind him. Once they were seated on a plank across the wagon box, Papa sliced the fruit into narrow bands. Sven bit into one. The juice filled his mouth with tangy sweetness, even better than the smell had been.

"Muskmelon good?" asked the farmer's son as he climbed up beside his father on the wagon seat.

"Muskmelon?" Papa said, trying the English word. "Ya, good."

Sven finished his slice and reached for another, but Papa handed it to the farmer's son.

The boy shook his head. He spoke in English, but Sven knew he wasn't hungry. He was waiting for supper at home.

"Muskmelon." Sven repeated the word until he knew he would not forget it. One English word. He wished he knew how to say *milk* and *potatoes* and *meat* and *pie*. He was hungry enough, even after eating half of that big fruit, to eat anything the farmer's wife might offer them for supper.

Neither the farmer nor his son tried to speak to them. Nor did they speak to each other, although they seemed cheerful enough. Mr. Schmidt was not as tall as Papa, though he was, like Papa, about thirty-five years old, Sven guessed. He was sunburned, and the hair on his exposed forearms was bleached almost white. His beard was a dull red. The son was younger than Sven, possibly eleven, maybe not more than ten. He wore no shoes. His bare legs were the color of his father's arms, a deep copper color.

Mile after mile with the horses stepping along at a good pace, the farmer drove down a road as straight as the edge of a board. Fields on either side of the road were golden green with wheat almost ripe. They passed orchards heavy with apples and pears still green, and peaches beginning to ripen gold. They passed trellised vines sagging with grapes. Nearly every farm had a potato field.

At last the wagon turned into a short lane toward a farmhouse. The farmer drove under a lean-to shed and stopped the horses.

"Come along," the boy called to Sven in English.

He ran ahead, and Sven ran to catch up, muttering, "Come along."

They were to draw water for the horses. Sven watched the boy bring up one bucketful with the windlass. "I'll do this," he said in Swedish. "My name's Sven. What's your name?"

"Otto," the boy said. He handed Sven the bucket and ran to the brick house.

Sven hauled up several buckets and poured the water into the trough for the horses. Finally, he put his mouth to the bucket's edge and took a long drink himself. Papa had helped Mr. Schmidt unhitch the horses. He led them now with a hand at each halter.

"I'll turn the potatoes out with the plow tomorrow," Papa said. "You and the boy will pick up potatoes in baskets."

"His name is Otto," Sven said. "Like Mama's brother."

"They're German," Papa said. "German isn't so different from Swedish. I know a few words of German and can piece together a little more. I suppose they use English with their children so they'll speak like Americans."

Sven walked with Papa to the barn, where they fed the horses and brushed them down.

"Come along, Anderson," Mr. Schmidt said.

"Come along," Sven repeated under his breath.

*   *   *   *

Mrs. Schmidt and four tall girls stood in a row behind a table loaded with vegetables and bread and meat. Beside each plate was a glassful of milk, and the clear glass pitcher of milk stood in the middle of the table.

"Wash here," Otto told Sven.

A white enameled pan was filled with water. Otto handed him a block of brown soap.

Papa and Mr. Schmidt washed, and after they were seated, Mrs. Schmidt and the girls sat down too. Mr. Schmidt dropped his head. Sven guessed he was praying, but he wasn't sure whether in German or English.

Sven opened his eyes.

"Bread?" Mrs. Schmidt held out a plate toward him.

He looked at her and smiled. "Bread," he repeated in English. "Thanks."

He took a slice and passed the plate to Papa.

"Corn?" Mrs. Schmidt held out a blue bowl piled high.

"Corn?" He took a hot golden cylinder in his hand and set it quickly on his plate. "Thanks."

He recognized the beans, and he repeated the English word after Mrs. Schmidt. He took cucumbers and beets and cabbage and meat.

The English words were becoming a jumble in his memory. Finally, everything was passed, and he set to eating, glad that the muskmelon had not dulled his appetite.

They would sleep on narrow iron beds filled with straw tick in the loft over the granary. The place was clean. The beds were freshly made. Sven went to sleep before he had time to enjoy the miracle of a real bed.

* * * * *

After a breakfast of oatmeal and cream, eggs, and toast with butter, Sven went to the potato field. Papa guided the plow carefully down a row of potato plants. Behind him the upturned earth was speckled with large white potatoes, their skins still thin because they were not yet ripe. Sven let Otto start, then went ahead a few yards, straddled the row, and bent over. When the basket filled, he poured the potatoes into a burlap bag and moved on. Otto emptied his basket into the bag and moved ahead. After digging three long rows, Papa took the team and plow back to the barn lot. When he returned, he started picking up potatoes on the far end of the field.

The sun was hot. Sven had been idle for so long aboard the ship and then on the train that he ached from the work by midmorning. But Otto's oldest sister came with cold water and bread and butter. Then Sven was almost as glad Papa had found Mr. Schmidt as he had been when he got into bed the night before. He practiced the English words in his head. *Bread. Butter. Water. Drink.*

Returning to the house for the noon meal, they passed the kitchen garden. A wooden wheelbarrow stood beside the path, piled high with muskmelons. Otto stopped, grasped the handles, and pushed the wheelbarrow at a trot along the fence toward the pigpen. He opened the gate and dumped the load into the pen. The fruits rolled across the muddy ground, and the pigs came grunting.

Sven was aghast. "Muskmelons good?"

"Too ripe," Otto said in English. "Too many. We can't eat them all. Everybody has too many muskmelons."

Sven did not grasp the full meaning, but he realized that Papa had paid too much for the muskmelon the day before. Even when they lived on the farm in Sweden, Sven had never seen such abundance. This was a rich land with rich, deep soil. It was much warmer than Sweden. When he sat up to the table for the noon dinner, he heartily wished he might stay here forever and never have to go to the pine forests and become a logger. And then he remembered that logging was only a way to earn a start. In two years he and Papa would have enough money to bring Mama and the younger children over from Sweden. Then they would have their own farm, and if they worked hard, they, too, would enjoy riches such as this.

He asked Mrs. Schmidt for paper. He labored several nights writing a letter to Mama. Mrs. Schmidt helped him address it to Grandfather Oldstrom's home in Sweden, and she posted the letter. Mrs. Schmidt did not know that Papa could not write, and he could read only a few words in Swedish. Mrs. Schmidt did not know that Mama would have Lesja read the letter aloud, for Mama had not been to school herself. In their youth, his parents had lived on isolated farms in the countryside. Sven and Lesja had profited at least in going to school when they moved to the city tenement.

CHAPTER 2

From South Bend to Pinch River

They worked through mid-October for Mr. Schmidt, harvesting potatoes, wheat, then field corn. During that time they ate better than Sven could remember ever eating before. They learned English and went to church with the Schmidts on Sunday. When a book salesman passed through, Mrs. Schmidt bought a book illustrated with pictures of strange animals with wings and horns. After the noon meal, while the men stretched out in the shade to rest for a half hour, Otto brought out the book and began teaching Sven to read English from the book. Sven was surprised that many words that sounded very different in English looked on paper very much like the Swedish word for the same idea. He could skim along through a page telling about a prophecy in the Bible and get the general meaning. He didn't know much about the Bible because his family had never attended church back home in Sweden, but he was too tired after work in the fields to play. Learning to read English would be useful.

Mr. Schmidt paid Papa on October 21 at the bank in South Bend. They bought boots and socks, long-handled underwear and woolen pants, mittens and mackinaws. Papa saved as much as possible, for he knew from Mr. Schmidt that they would not be paid until summer for the timber work, which would end in April. Sven wrote another letter to Mama and mailed it.

That same day they boarded the train for the timber country in northern Michigan using the passes Papa had received when he signed on with McEllroy's.

The train, to Sven's surprise, would not take them to their destination.

"Logs come out of this country by the rivers," another Swede told them after they boarded the train. "We take the rails to Grand Rapids. After that it's by ox stage or on our own hooves." He laughed and stamped his heavy boots on the floor. "A man walks a good deal in the pineries. We walk out of camp with a full belly before first light every morning, and saws start singing before sunrise. Got to make every minute count on short winter days. We walk back to camp after dark so cold our feet don't want to move."

"Back in Sweden, loggers use sets of wheels to get the timber out in the summer," Papa said. "Why not here?"

"Ya, sure, I remember how it's done," the man said. "You cut a log as big as your oxen can handle, and you raise up the front end and chain it so it swings from the underside of the big axle. Once the oxen start it rolling, it's going to keep rolling unless they ram into a stump or hit uneven ground. But here we have rivers."

Sven looked at Papa. *As if there were no rivers in Sweden.*

"This land's never been logged before," the man said. "Wait until you see these white pines!"

* * * *

Before the train ride ended in Grand Rapids, Sven and Papa had talked to all the men in their car. Many of them were veterans of several years in the woods, some even experienced on the rivers of Maine on the Atlantic seacoast. They were all a shabby and tattered lot. They were loud and friendly. They were proud of their strength, proud of how they endured hardships, even proud of the danger of their work and the near-death accidents they had survived. What mattered most were the rough, manly loyalties that developed in the camps.

Sven tried to picture the winter's work as the men described it. There would be a big cookshack, made of rough lumber. Inside, wooden tables would seat a hundred or more men. At each place would be a tin plate, a cup, and fork and spoon. The cook and his helpers would set food on each table.

"Don't you talk at table," one logger warned Sven. "Just wolf down your beans and bread and get out of there. Cooks don't stand for talk at table."

"Food's good, though," a teamster named Bates said. "A man needs the best grub he can get if he has to work that hard in the cold."

There would be a long bunkhouse with shelves, usually four high, on both sides onto which men crawled to sleep. A fire burned hot all night, but except for those in bunks nearby, the loggers generated their own heat like so many cattle in a barn.

Loggers were ranked by their job. The sawyers felled the giant pines with crosscut saws. Swampers followed them with double-bitted axes, cutting off the limbs. Buckers cut the long trunk into logs ten, twelve, or sixteen feet long. Skidders backed a draft horse close enough to hitch a chain to the log so it could be yarded. Soon a teamster brought up a double bobsled that would be loaded ten feet high with logs. When the load was chained securely, the huge draft horses would pull the load downhill on icy tracks to the edge of the river or a lake. All winter long, yarders built the piles of timber near the ice. In the spring when the ice broke through and the river began to flow, drivers guided the timber downstream to a sawmill town or sometimes even to Lake Michigan or Lake Superior.

Sven had not seen a map of northern Michigan. He hadn't even seen a map of the United States since they left Sweden. He tried to imagine mountainsides covered with tall pines and rivers flowing into lakes that the loggers said were as big as the sea.

The logging company had hired Sven, and Papa had said he could do the work, but Sven couldn't imagine what work he would be assigned. It all sounded like work for men, not boys.

* * * * *

As they continued to travel north, they came to hills, but no mountains, not even when they entered pine forests. Beyond the rails, the loggers loaded equipment onto wagons, and the caravan moved farther north into unsettled land.

"It's a band of white pine fifty miles wide running up the eastern shore of Lake Michigan," a Swede returning to the camps for his third season told Sven's father. "Once the timber's off, it will make great farmland. Folks are standing in line to buy it up before we pull out. Pinch River Camp is in new territory. They'll have enough ground cleared for the big shanty and maybe the walls up. But they brought us here before the snows to get a roof on the bunkhouse and put up the cookshack and the store."

The Swede looked at Sven with a critical eye. "You can't be fourteen years old."

Sven ignored the statement.

"Don't lie," Papa had said. "But just jump to do whatever job they give you and stand as tall as you can. Act like a man, and you'll pass for fourteen."

In Stockholm, Sven had seemed taller than other boys his age. But as he tramped along the road to the new logging camp, Sven felt small. And he was the only immigrant boy, though there were adult Swedes and Poles and Scots, an Irishman, and even an Italian, all trying to understand each other in their few newly acquired English words. The boys were American born and proud that they were.

Like the men, the boys spoke with a variety of accents that made their English more difficult to understand. Like the men, the boys wore patched and threadbare clothing. They limped in broken-down boots that were too small for their growing feet. Their sleeves came just past their elbows, and their shirts stretched tight across muscular shoulders.

There were nine other boys, and without a doubt, they were all older than the required fourteen. All were returning veteran swampers but one. Bill Sutherland was a cookee and wore a black bowler hat to make sure the other shanty boys showed him due respect.

Arnie Bledsoe was a loudmouthed sixteen-year-old who claimed he was from a farm near Battle Creek.

Sam Duell and his half brother Bobby Cooper were from Battle Creek as well and knew Arnie. They were both quiet but stuck to each other like cockleburs.

Noodge McUftee with his dark-brown curly hair was from Allegan.

Bjarnie Syvertson looked like a Swede and sounded like one. But when Sven spoke to him in Swedish, he didn't understand. His father had been born in Detroit.

Jamie Laughton bragged he was born in a logging camp in New York.

Raf van Ryke was a Hollander from a farm on the Lake Michigan shore.

Isaiah Green was the oldest, eighteen, and tough enough that Arnie shut his mouth when Isaiah said to.

Sven was certain there wasn't a boy among them who would want to be his friend. If he had any friends at all, he would have to work on the men who had sons of their own and had a feeling for a boy his age. But then it would be a shameful thing for a boy nearly man-grown to look for pity among the men with soft hearts.

The first night on the road with the wagons, the full moon came up before they pulled off into a clearing.

"This is Pinch River," Arnie hollered.

"We seen Pinch River last year going out," Jamie Laughton snapped. "You ain't the only shanty boy with sawdust in your long-handles."

The teamsters unhitched the horses.

Sven saw the driver take the first team to a shallow pool at the edge of the stream to drink.

"I'll take your horses," he offered the teamster named Bates who had been talking to Papa earlier.

He took the reins Bates handed him and put the bay team in line.

Bates was munching on an apple when Sven brought the team to him. He tied the horses beyond the wagons and gave them their nose bags. "You like horses?"

"Papa had horses when I was little," Sven said, remembering the dappled mares they had left behind on the farm when Uncle Jens took over the homestead. The horses had, of course, belonged to Grandfather Anderson before he died.

"Horses are important in logging," Mr. Bates said. "We take as good care of them as we do the men. Maybe better. Then, some of the horses got more sense than some of the men got." He laughed and clapped his hand on the shoulder of the near horse. "For certain, there's not a man in camp that works as hard as my team. Wait until you see the loads these girls can pull out of the woods."

The cook had gone ahead and had supper ready, boiled beans with salt pork and molasses, scalding hot coffee, and store-bought bread.

"You won't get none of that after breakfast tomorrow," Noodge McUftee told Sven. "Cookee bought up fifty loaves of day-old from the baker in Grand Rapids to make do until he gets to camp and sets up his stovepipe. Then it will be pancakes with molasses or baking powder biscuits with butter. I saw them loading the food wagons. Two washtubs of butter to start with."

Sven rolled out his blanket next to Papa and slept on the ground. The earth was dry under the pines. A soft wind blew. The full moon shone through a gap in the woods where the stream curved and flowed west. He was almost asleep when an owl hooted. He jolted awake for an instant then drifted off again.

* * * * *

They had fresh sausage and bread and coffee for breakfast. They hiked beside the wagons for twenty miles. The road was little more than wagon tracks following Pinch River through almost solid shade. Just before dark, they came into the unfinished camp. This time there were boiled potatoes with the boiled beans, more store-bought bread with butter—and coffee.

"I heard they're bringing in five milk cows," Raf said after pouring part of his coffee into the bark and pine needles on the ground. "I heard they hired two men to put up hay last summer on a beaver meadow up the river from camp."

"Aw, they always make hay for the horses," Arnie said. "My brother hires on every summer after he gets Pa's hay made." Bobby's left eyebrow signaled a question. "Arnie's mother and father died in a fire winter before last," he muttered in Sven's ear. "He never did have a brother."

There was some talk among the farm boys about mosquitoes and no-see-ums, which Sven took to be some kind of stinging insects that swarmed over hay meadows in summer.

They reached camp just before dark. Sven again helped Bates with the horses, leading them to water first, then up a trail to the edge of a hay meadow where a rail fence enclosed a paddock.

The log walls of the shanty that would become a bunkhouse for the loggers had been raised about five feet. After three days, the loggers had brought the walls up another three logs, had strung pole rafters that rested on a long ridge pole, which, in turn, rested on the trunks of pine trees that had been topped and limbed, but stood where they grew. Planks and rolled tar paper had been hauled in for the roof. With broadaxes, the men hewed timbers to support the planks on which the men would sleep. The bunks were three high, just shelves. Sven discovered that shanty boys were expected to take the top bunks.

"They're still half squirrel," one lumberjack said as he stowed his duffle in the spot he had claimed.

"That's not so bad," Raf confided. "When real cold sets in and they keep a roaring fire in the barrel stove, it's warmer under the roof."

Breakfast, dinner, and supper, Bill Sutherland and the bull cook[1] boiled huge pots of beans and fried potatoes with onions in skillets

---

1. The "bull cook" was the camp tender, who cut fuel, filled wood boxes, swept bunkhouses, and did a variety of other tasks.

nearly two feet across—all over outdoor fires carefully laid and carefully controlled. The bull cook had a lot to say about getting the cookshack built, and a crew of choppers and hewers set about that job right away.

*   *   *   *   *

For four days, Sven ran whatever errand the camp foreman yelled for. Then he, along with Sam and Bobby and Noodge, was sent with the teamster, Bates, and a crew of seven loggers to clear a road between the camp and the landing where the logs would be yarded. The road would cover a distance of four miles over almost flat ground along a shallow valley that Sven guessed was a creek bed in rainy weather.

Bates pointed out peeled sapling stakes that marked the course the road should follow. A few medium to large pines or hardwoods needed to be cut. Experienced loggers set about felling and bucking these. Noodge, with his double-bladed ax, was their swamper.

"You, Bobby, show Sven and Sam how to clear out the brush so we won't have stubs to injure the horses' hooves."

"Pay attention," Bobby warned, "where the fellers are and what direction they plan to bring their tree down. And know before they yell where you want to run. When they call out *TIMBER*, you don't have much time to think."

Sven watched how Bobby pulled a small maple sapling with one remaining scarlet leaf to the side until earth around its roots began to rise up.

"See where the roots is?" Bobby chopped into the earth once for each of three roots and pulled away the sapling. "It's tough on axes, but the filer's got a grindstone we keep whirring."

Sven took up his ax and grabbed an oak as big around as his thumb. When he pulled, there were no lines in the leaf mold showing where the roots spread.

"It's got a taproot," Bobby said. "Just chop it once below ground level.

"Pile all the brush out of the roadway," Bobby said. He left Sam and Sven and trotted off to carry away limbs for the swampers.

When Sven looked ahead an hour later, he saw a trail opening a quarter mile ahead, a few logs along one edge, and only three stumps in the path. The swampers had set to chopping large roots around the first, rather the same way Bobby had showed the boys how to cut the roots from saplings. Sven watched them loop a chain under the edge of a severed root, then around the stump. Bates hitched his team to the stump. The horses pulled first one direction and then another until the stump began to rock, and the earth fell away from other roots. Swampers chopped a few more roots, and then the team jerked twice. The stump rolled from its hole, and they pulled it off the road. Noodge took up a shovel and filled the hole with soil and small rock, patted the surface smooth, and trotted to the next stump. Bobby's arm signal clearly meant, "Get back to work!"

While Sven could cut more than a hundred saplings while the fellers brought down one large tree, he figured there must be thousands of bushes and baby trees for every big one in the roadway. He wasn't paying enough attention to the fellers when their next big one swayed and started down.

"TIMBER!" the logger shouted.

Sven looked up to see the tree coming back through the opening cleared for the road. He leaped three long bounds into the woods to the right just as pine limbs splintered and the slender upper trunk crashed to the earth. A few seconds before, he had been pulling on a seven-foot aspen where the pine's trunk now lay. His legs trembling, Sven waded through the broken brittle limbs to locate his ax. What if its handle had been broken?

He looked around to see if Sam had noticed his close call, but Sam was coming in from the left of the tree, his ax in hand. Together they began slicing off the small upper limbs from the trunk and throwing them onto their brush pile off the roadway. Two buckers measured off three long logs then made their cuts with a long saw they pulled back and forth between them.

"They won't even use this part," Sam said after a few minutes.

Sven took his cue and slashed the rest of the top into pieces he could carry away and went back to cutting brush. Bates pulled the logs off to a pile farther down.

"You boys holding up?" he asked.

"I'm fine," Sam said.

Sven grinned, but he wasn't fine. His knees were still full of jelly after the close call with the pine tree.

*　*　*　*　*

There was drinking water from a can with a dipper, and Sven drank a lot, but he was hungry long before the bull cook's horn sounded for dinner. Back in camp he grabbed the filled tin plate Bill Sutherland handed him and found a stump where he sat to wolf down his food. He knew he was expected back on the trail job when the horn sounded at the end of an hour.

When Sven finished, he spread his feet to stand up, but the seat of his pants stuck to the pine resin on the stump. He was glad no one was looking at him. With a lunge he was free of the stump. He took his plate to the tub of hot soapy water and dropped it in.

"You ready?" Sam asked.

"Say, Cooper," Arnie Bledsoe called out to Bobby as they set out from camp, "does that yellow-haired Swede kid know which end of the ax is the handle?"

"He'll do," Bobby said without smiling.

Sven wondered if Bobby thought he was a slow worker. He determined to build up his speed, just as he had in Schmidt's potato and corn fields. But here he had to remember timber coming down while he worked as fast as he could.

At least I'm strong, Sven thought.

By the time the roadway was cleared to the lakeshore, Sven had learned how to cut and stack brush as rapidly as Bobby did, how to scramble with his ax in his hand before the word *TIMBER* left the feller's mouth, how to observe what was happening all along the line while paying close attention to what he himself was doing. He thought Sam was probably his friend, but Sam was always so quiet that it was hard to tell.

Sven liked Bates. He was pretty sure Bates liked boys in general, but maybe Sven Anderson in particular.

Since leaving Sweden, he had tried to push memories of his family's beloved faces from his mind, or at least into a corner, until bedtime. Then, when the loggers and the other boys settled into their straw-tick beds and snores rumbled from the half-open mouths of heavy sleepers, he had indulged the heartache that had only grown worse with the passing months. Worst of all, he couldn't remember how his tiny brother had looked, mostly just a mewing little bundle Mama kept always near her breast, wrapped in her shawl. Now the baby would be standing on his feet, with Lesja and Karen holding his hands and walking him about Grandfather's small whitewashed rooms.

Sven dreamed of land of their own where he and Papa cut tall pines and brought them to a small clearing in the forest. In those dreams Sven peeled the smooth logs and Papa notched them. They raised the walls and framed in doorways and windows with finished lumber. They put up rafters and nailed on roofing boards and then cedar shingles. They finished the floor with smooth pine boards and put glass in the window openings. They hung doors at the front of the log house and where the kitchen opened on a small vegetable garden with potatoes and carrots and beets and cabbages and muskmelons.

And the beautiful dream only made his heart ache the more. What if he and Papa could not after all save enough money to buy a farm and pay ocean passage and train fare to bring Mama and the other children to it? Six months had passed since they left Stockholm.

CHAPTER 3

From Boots
to Body Lice

In the whole week they had been working on the sled road, Sven had hardly seen Papa. Papa, while not an experienced lumberman, had cut timber on the farm in Sweden and for one season in the mountains when he was a youth. Most important, he had experience building with pine logs and was an expert at notching corners. The camp foreman had put Papa in charge of building the cookshack. When the walls were up for that building, the foreman moved him to construct the camp store, which was to be only twelve by sixteen feet.

The shanty boys were especially interested in the camp store.

"Boots is what I want," Noodge said.

"I'm gonna get me a whole outfit right off," Arnie Bledsoe said. "Two of everything." He looked at Sven. "How come you bought everything spanking new before we started work? Your granddad the king of Sweden?"

"I worked in harvest," Sven said. "Papa said we needed outfits."

"Didn't we all?" muttered Arnie.

"Shut your big mouth, Arnie," Isaiah said.

Sven held his breath, expecting Arnie to take a swing at Isaiah.

"Oh, Isaiah cleaned his face last winter," Bobby said in a whisper. "Arnie don't talk smart to Isaiah. He's got a good memory."

34

When he came to camp each noon, Sven saw what Papa was accomplishing. But Papa was too busy earning a reputation for himself as a broadaxman to see the skills Sven had learned. Other workers had put roofs on the shacks, and Papa had begun a shop for the blacksmith and the filer to share.

* * * * *

The second Sunday in camp, the superintendent of the whole McEllroy operation rode in on a long-legged dapple gray mare. He inspected the store building and ordered an iron bedstead set up at the end of the counter.

After breakfast, the bull cook blew his short horn before the meal was finished. "If every logger heaves to for a half hour, we can have all my supplies and equipment into the cook shanty. There'll be apple pie if some fool don't lose my pie tins."

The cookshack had a plank floor. Now men reassembled long plank tables and benches. Others carried in metal or wooden barrels containing lard, flour, sugar, and molasses. Sven carried in twenty-six wooden boxes of dried fruit—prunes, apricots, peaches, raisins, and apples. Barrels of salt pork were rolled on planks off the grub wagons and through the cookshack door, where Bill Sutherland began stacking the boxes of fruit on all but one of them.

Bates pulled the empty wagons back along the edge of the trail that had brought them into camp along Pinch River.

"Tomorrow he'll drive back to Grand Rapids for another load of food," Raf told Sven. "When the snow builds up, they can bring in supplies on sleds, but it's best to have as much as they can here before it gets that cold. The cook's the most important man in a logging camp. More important than the bull boss."

Sven grinned. "Is that because men work better when they like the food?"

Raf nodded toward Bill Sutherland in his black bowler hat. "Bill's planning to cook for the log drive in June. He'll have to rustle meals better'n anything we get here and all out of a wanigan—that's a cookshack on a small raft. The river pigs get good pay, but they risk breaking legs or getting smashed every day of the drive. The cook never leaves the wanigan, and the only danger he risks is disappointed drivers. But he'll get paid more'n anybody else in the drive, and there's not a man on the drive that complains of that."

The crew drifted away from the cookshack, and Sven and Sam found Bobby boiling his underwear and socks in a small iron barrel. Sam cut a maple pole and peeled it. Sven watched him fish his brother's clothes from the scalding water into a shallow pan. While Bobby took his things to the riverside to rinse in the cold water, Sam dropped his dirty clothes into the barrel and stirred them around.

"There's strong brown soap we brought from home in there," he said. "You want to use the water when I get done with it? Bobby says it's the only way to keep down the louse population."

"You got bit by any bedbugs yet?" Jamie Laughton asked in passing.

"None yet," Sam said.

"They hasn't found us yet," Jamie said. "I'll give 'em until Friday."

"Bedbugs?" Sven had heard of folks in Sweden with bedbugs in their houses. Such people were looked upon as unfit company, even in the public school. Like children with head lice.

Arnie Bledsoe kicked a fire log and sent ashes in a cloud around the barrel of boiling clothes. "Bedbugs? Head lice? Body lice? You ain't never been bit? I seen Swedes bit up scalp to toenails just like the rest of us."

Sven felt like socking Arnie, but thought better. Arnie was twenty pounds heavier and a lot tougher. *Let the bedbugs devour him skin and bones,* he thought, and took some comfort in just thinking it.

He helped Sam get his clothes out of the hot water, and though it now looked rather like bubbling brown broth, he stirred his own dirty clothes into the barrel and kept on stirring while Sam swished one garment after another in the water flowing swiftly over the rocks at the edge of Pinch River. When Sam had wrung out his last sock, Sven called for the flat pan.

"I had better hurry before Gabriel blows!"

He had his clothes out and halfway to the stream when the bull cook blew the seven-foot tin horn for dinner. Sven set the pan under the low branches of a hemlock and ran to the cookshack, still wiping his wet arms on the front of his shirt. He was surprised to be the first person in, but he took a seat in the middle of the bench of the middle table, facing the stove so he could see the food coming. The shanty boys and the loggers lined up at the door and filed in, every man choosing his place and sitting down only after careful consideration.

Papa came in near the end of the line, but he came to sit beside Sven.

"I washed my clothes," Sven said in Swedish. "Bobby and Sam had soap from home. I used their hot water. My things will bear long rinsing, but I boiled them a good while. Papa, will there really be bedbugs?"

"I should think so," Papa said. He did not seem concerned. "Somebody is sure to bring some in on their blankets. They'll spread. Boiling your clothes will help with the lice, but the bedbugs—you can't get rid of them."

*   *   *   *   *

Monday Bates set out for Grand Rapids with each shanty boy who knew how to drive a team in charge of a wagon. Sven was glad he'd learned to handle horses at the Schmidts' farm during the late summer. They reached Grand Rapids at midday the second day, loaded supplies, and set out north again. Instead of camping that night, they stopped in a farmyard. The farm wife fed them, and the farmer sent them to the hayloft to sleep, high against the rafters on top of the winter's supply of clover hay.

When he harnessed his team in the morning, Sven saw Bates leading two cream-colored cows from the barn. Behind him, the farmer led a red cow with a splotch of white running like spilled paint down her face and neck and a black cow with a white saddle. Bates tied one cow to the back of each of four wagons, including Sven's.

"Keep the horses moving slowly enough so the cow won't have to trot to keep up," Bates said.

"See, I was right," Raf said.

"You said there'd be five," Arnie reminded him.

"Two is Jerseys, and that counts double on the cream," Raf said with a grin and a shrug. "And the big Friesian counts double on the amount she'll give, so I guess we're taking back seven cows."

"Then you and Yellow-hair get to milk them if you know so much about cows," Arnie shouted as he climbed on the seat of the wagon he was to drive.

"Ya, sure," Sven called back to Raf. "And I'll help you." He had learned to milk when he was a very small child, and if he and Papa bought a farm, cows would be an important part of their living. He noticed that though Arnie had often bragged about his father's successful farm in Battle Creek, Bates had not tied a cow to Arnie's wagon.

With the cows holding them to a slow walk, they were late arriving back at Pinch River Camp. They left the wagons beside the cookshack, unhitched the horses, and walked them up the short trail toward the rail-fenced lot near the hay meadow where they were kept. In the shadows Sven saw a low structure where there had been none four days before.

Coming closer, he saw it was a pole shed roofed over with coarse hay.

"Each team will have its own stall," Bates said. "Make sure you always get them in the right place. Horses are peculiar about that."

After the horses were settled with hay and grain, Sven went back with Bates and Raf to bring down the cows.

"Cows are even more peculiar than horses," Bates said. "They won't even go into a stall that belongs to another cow."

Sven wondered whether cows and horses knew about bedbugs or whether bedbugs bothered livestock. He thought, as he went to his supper in the cookshack, that the next day was Friday. Jamie had given the bedbugs until Friday to find every bed in the bunkhouse.

He ate the cold beans and biscuits Bill Sutherland had set back for their supper. Tomorrow there would be milk.

But when Sven was finished with the cold supper, Bill Sutherland was at the cookshack door with four three-gallon buckets.

"Sven, your dad says you can milk, and Raf sure can. Go along, lads. Bates is down there already with a lantern."

"Well, they won't give much after hoofing it all day," Raf prophesied.

He was right. There was cream for the coffee in the morning and one mug of milk for each man at lunch. But with good feed and time to chew their cuds in their pole barn, the cows filled the pails Friday night.

Sven had forgotten that this was Jamie's deadline for the arrival of the bedbugs. He slept peacefully in his top bunk at the end of the shanty, unaware that snow was falling in a heavy blanket on the pine forest.

* * * * *

Morning marked the beginning of November, and cream on oatmeal porridge and apricot cobbler with cream and mugsful of milk for anyone who wanted it.

"My mother won't let me drink coffee at home," Raf said. "If she knew we gets coffee three times a day in the camp, she'd never let me come." He grinned. "If she knew they'd feed me pie twice a day, she'd keep me home—say I'd get too spoiled to live in the same house with the rest of 'em."

Sven wondered if Mama and Lesja and the little ones had enough to eat at Grandpa Oldstrom's house. Grandpa lived at the edge of the city and grew a large garden. But he had no income except the small pension awarded him for his wounds in defending Sweden in a war long ago in his youth. The pension was enough for the old man to live with dignity in the house he had inherited from his own grandfather, but it was certainly not enough to keep growing children supplied with wholesome food. Perhaps, Sven thought, Lesja had quit school to keep the little ones so Mama could work in a great house as laundress or cook. He wondered if Lesja had milk to pour into mugs for the little ones each morning. He wondered if they had bread and cabbage. He was certain they had no meat or eggs.

"I never ate beans three times a day in my life," he told Raf. "But, then I never had pie except on Sunday, either."

Sunday the bull cook spread a light meal for noon, though the cookshack smelled of apples and cinnamon.

"The big crew comes in before dark," Bobby said when they put their tin plates in the washtub after eating. "Bill's been rolling pie dough since breakfast, and the oven's been full. This camp has a reputation for good grub. They're bound to live up to it from the start."

Several teamsters came into camp with planks across their bob-sleds and twenty men riding in each.

When the horn sounded for supper, the new men crowded into the cookshack, and two tables, where the early crew ate, were filled with regular crew. Sven shrugged and took an empty place at a different table. He'd get his usual place back next time.

Talk wasn't allowed at the table, but the superintendent stood up to make a speech when every logger had a plate and before anybody thought of leaving.

"Breakfast will start at four. That means the shanty is quiet and dark at nine. We'll fill you up with the best food you'll find in any logging camp in Michigan. The cookee will bring flaggins to the woods at noon. We'll work until it's too dark to see a horse from a tree. We'll come to supper when Gabriel blows at seven. Never heard no complaints on the bull cook's biscuits or sausage and gravy. What about his pie?"

The loggers looked up from their plates. A few old hands cheered, but new loggers couldn't bring themselves to break the rule for silence in the cookshack. Counting the superintendent, who was standing but had a place, Sven counted twelve men at each table. There were nine tables. The bull cook and Bill Sutherland were on their feet carrying bowls full of food to the men. A hundred and ten men at Pinch River Camp.

"We've got some of the best white pine timber in the world right here on Pinch River," the superintendent continued. "We've got top-notch fellers and buckers and the best teamsters in the state. We aim to take out every sawlog in hauling distance before spring break-up, and we aim to have more board feet per man than any other camp on the Lake Michigan watershed.

"There's a blacksmith to keep the horses shod and to fix any equipment that breaks down. There's a man at the grindstone sharpening half the axes every day and filing saws. We've enough spare ax handles to replace three for every man here before spring, but don't break none just to show you can chop that hard. The company store is open Sunday afternoons. You all have your jobs assigned. Finish that pie and be here at four in the morning."

The next day the real work began. Sven was almost glad he had been assigned to be a stable boy for morning chores, including morning milking, cleaning the stable, and filling all the mangers with hay. After the noon meal, he would go to the woods as a swamper, and Raf would feed, water, and milk the cows, curry the horses when the teams came in, and feed them their oats—all before Gabriel blew the supper horn. When Sven got to the shanty, a logger with a red sash tied around his middle was playing a fiddle next to the barrel stove. A man down the way cupped a harmonica between his hands, and two Irishmen were jigging under the lantern. Sven slipped behind the barrel stove, sat down on the edge of the bottom bunk to take off his boots, then climbed to his place on the top bunk. He crawled between his blankets and closed his eyes. The Irishmen's boots were stamping to the fiddle tune when he fell asleep.

Sven was out of his bunk and washed before Gabriel blew the horn at 4:00 A.M. He was also the first person in line at the cookshack door. When Bill Sutherland opened it, Sven went to his usual place at the second table and sat down. Five minutes later a logger with red suspenders stopped beside him.

"That's my place you're sitting in," he said.

"It's mine," Sven said. "I've been sitting here for three weeks."

"I sat there last night. That's what counts for the season," the logger said. "Get up and move on."

"No," Sven said, though he said it mildly.

The logger gripped him by the collar and pulled him from the bench and chunked him to the floor. Sven sprang up and socked the middle-aged logger in the middle because that was where his fist happened to land. The logger slugged him an awful one in the jaw.

"Stop that!" the bull cook yelled. "Take that fight outside!"

Sven got up slowly and found another place at the table. The logger in the red suspenders sat down, and breakfast was served.

"Should have warned you," Bates said later as he hitched up his team. "Places at table is sacred territory. If Harrington had given up his place, not a logger in the bunch would have any respect for him. Remember the spot you got when Harrington finished with you, for that's your spot at table until the camp breaks up in the spring."

Sven milked all four cows, carried two trips of milk to the cookshack, cleaned the stalls where the horses had spent the night, and put refuse hay under the cows once their stalls were cleaned. He filled all the mangers with fresh hay and led each cow to the river to drink. He harnessed the one team assigned for the cookee. There was no clock to tell him the time, but he washed his face and hands and went to the shanty. He stretched out on his bunk to rest. He was just dozing when Bill Sutherland opened the shanty door.

"Bring up the team."

The sled was already loaded with huge pots straight off the stove.

Sven hitched the team to the sled and climbed up. Bill blew for the noon meal.

This was the first day of the logging season, and as Sven guessed, the pattern would hold pretty true throughout the winter. It was a full week before bedbugs arrived in his bunk. But he was too tired each night to let them keep him awake. He was too tired to lie in his bunk remembering Mama and the younger children or to build the log house in his mind and furnish it with a table and benches and beds and cupboards. Sometimes he dreamed of the family far away, but most often he dreamed of the falling timber and the shouts of the swampers as they rushed in with their axes.

Like everyone else, Sven had lice in his underwear, and they kept him itching every waking hour. There wasn't much time to scratch, but like all the other boys and men, he did a good bit of it.

CHAPTER 4

From Rookie to Shanty Boy

Though Sunday afternoon was supposed to be store hours, the company store opened right after supper the first three nights the full crew was in camp. Men and boys lined up to buy new outfits, everything from socks and boots to mackinaws and mittens. Sven was shocked when he saw that nobody paid for the new gear. They just asked for what they needed, the clerk set it on the plank counter and wrote it all in his account book.

"It comes out of our wages," Jamie explained to Sven while the boys lounged around the stove watching the filer sharpen a saw. "It's like getting paid before we even start to work."

"If you spend your wages before you earn them, what do you get when work is over in the spring?" Sven asked.

"Oh, a few dollars," Jamie said. "I find me a job with a rich farmer when we're done here and eat off his table and sleep in his shed through harvest. Then when work starts in the pineries, I come along and get me a new outfit and eat the bull cook's grub and sleep in a warm shanty through the winter."

"But how can you get ahead?" Sven said.

Jamie laughed. "Why should I save back and buy a farm or a house in town? I'll get killed before I turn twenty-five, I figure. Dad did. Granddad made it to thirty-two. They both of them left a wife and babies and a mortgage. Not me. Loggers don't have no business making plans. Never saw an old man who was a logger all his life."

"That's not true," Isaiah said. "The smart ones live."

"You saying my dad wasn't a good logger?" Jamie backed off and raised his fists.

"I'm saying you might live past twenty-five if you pay attention to falling timber." Isaiah walked away from Jamie's belligerent fists.

"Watch Isaiah," Bobby Cooper advised Jamie. "He's slow to bring up his knuckles, but you won't pick a second fight with him."

"My dad was a good logger," Jamie insisted.

"Ya, sure," Bjarnie Syvertson said. "And smart loggers die young along with the dumb ones. The dumb ones get the rest of us killed. Watch out for dumb loggers."

It was good advice. Sven had seen enough before the regular loggers came to camp to realize that a moment's carelessness could put watchful men in danger. He saw it happen again and again during the weeks of early winter.

A chopper got the wrong slant on his undercut. The tree swung as the fellers sawed toward the undercut. The tree split suddenly and nearly exploded as it fell. One feller was smacked in the face by a narrow band of flying wood. Another was knocked senseless and had to be hauled in a sled to Grand Rapids, along with a swamper with a broken arm and a bucker with a broken leg.

A chainer made a bad hitch on a load of logs, and the loader would have been crushed when the load shifted and crashed down. But he was standing next to the sled and fell flat on his face in the snow next to the sled runner. The logs jumped over him but crushed the teamster, who was standing, at that moment, with his back to the loaded sled. The chainer saw it all happen, but he was unhurt.

Sven had cut himself twice with his ax, and both times the foreman tied the wound so tightly that it healed.

Noodge McUftee had said, "My daddy told me when I hired on, 'Son, don't have no enemies in the lumber camps. That's where you need friends. You want every man and boy there glad you live and breathe.' "

In spite of his earlier fears, Sven had friends: quiet Sam Duell and his older half brother Bobby Cooper, who paid special attention to the younger boys whenever they started a new assignment; Raf van Ryke, who found the same pleasure in caring for the livestock that Sven did; Bill Sutherland, the cookee; and the teamster Bates, who took a fatherly interest in all the shanty boys. Papa slept on the bunk below Sven's, but except for a few brief words in Swedish before the lantern was blown out each night, they hardly spoke.

"You have to look out for yourself in a place like this if you expect the respect of the other loggers," Papa told him twice, as if he were trying to explain why he had become so distant. "If I look out for you, the other shanty boys will think you're a weakling and need coddling."

Sven had expected the teamster with the red suspenders to hold a grudge after the incident in the cookshack, but Harrington often stopped to talk when he came to harness his team after breakfast. He drove a pair of matched Clydesdales, almost black, with magnificent white stockings and white blazes. He noticed that Sven had washed and brushed the long ruff at their ankles.

"You keep their stall clean, so they don't get soiled to begin with," he said.

"I'm sorry about hitting you," Sven said.

Harrington laughed good-naturedly. "Women have their manners at tea parties and such. We have some rules of etiquette here too. It's a good thing to know the rules. Now you know that one."

"It was my place, though," Sven insisted. "Papa and I came with the setup crew. I sat in that place from the first day after the roof went on the cookshack."

"Then I apologize," the teamster said. "As far as I could see, I got here the first day of the season, and the place I took for my first meal was my place. But you were kinda like the settler that runs ahead of the government and stakes a claim on land before it's open for home-steaders."

Sven didn't understand.

Harrington explained. "Any American man who claims one hundred sixty acres homestead land and improves it—lives on it for five years—gets a free title from the government. Not just everywhere, of course, but plenty of good land. You aim to be a farmer?"

"I do," Sven said.

"Then don't charge much at the company store," Harrington advised. "When paychecks come out in the spring, you'll have something to put away. When you're twenty-one and old enough to file on a homestead, you'll have your own stake."

"Papa and I want to bring Mama and the others over in two years," Sven confided.

The teamster shook his head. "It's a great dream, but it's hard for loggers to make much headway. They work so hard they feel like they deserve some fun when they get paid out in May or June. I wish you and your papa well, but it will be hard."

It was Papa's business, so Sven said nothing about it. But he knew Papa had put back money from the farmwork at the Schmidts' to take care of them through the winter and spring. They had their room and board as long as they were in camp, and they had their wages: forty dollars a month for Papa since he was a skilled hewer, and fifteen dollars a month for Sven. They would work at least five months. He did the arithmetic in his head. If they charged nothing against their wages, they would come out of camp in April with two hundred and seventy-five dollars. Maybe more. He was already making plans to ask Bates about letting him help with horses during the log drive.

* * * * *

Most of the loggers had been in the camps since they had turned fourteen. Like the shanty boys Sven knew best, they came from different situations. Sven saw one bucker reading the Bible. More often it was a tattered newspaper some new man had brought when he came into camp. Most of them chewed tobacco. Most of them had a bottle of whiskey hidden somewhere. Most of the loggers were highly skilled, very fast workers. If they weren't, they bragged a lot and hoped the other men would think they were. They loved to tell tall tales about their own wonderful deeds in other camps, and they loved to make up tales about logging heroes—former foremen, legendary cooks, historic log drives. Every night after supper, stories and fiddle music filled the shanty.

Most of the loggers were young men. Most of them were single. Within two weeks Sven also realized that most of them could explode in a minute like a tree that had barber-chaired. The loggers had knives and guns, but in the camp fights generally meant fists. When a fist fight broke out, the other men backed up and let the fighters finish what they started any way they could. The loser generally stuffed his gear into his bag and left camp. If a logger got fed up with getting less respect than he thought was his due, he, too, grabbed his bag and left. When the foreman came down hard on a man who wasn't learning logging as fast as he should, the newcomer walked off. A new man showed up in the shanty almost every night, someone to replace an injured man or a quitter.

Sven was proud that Papa was respected in Pinch River Camp. Papa was learning how to fit in with the seasoned loggers. He began to walk with the certain swagger and talk with the certain bluff loudness so different from his old ways. But Papa was earning good pay, and the other men sometimes stood around something he was building just to see how he did it.

"Got to hand it to you, Anderson," Sven heard a logger with a blond beard comment. "You can join corners so tight not a breath of a draft can come in. You're the best man I ever saw with a broadax."

* * * * *

After cutting himself twice with his ax, Sven concentrated on perfecting his swing.

"Stand on the other side of the log," Bobby told him. "Keep the tree trunk between you and your blade." He demonstrated the angle and the rhythm of a good swamper.

Sven was learning to slice off limbs, sometimes two at a swipe. He was waiting when his feller yelled "TIMBER," out of danger's way, but ready to leap in with his ax and clear the way for his buckers. By the time they finished their last cut, he was watching the feller again, ready. If the next tree took longer than usual, he might have time to watch the skidder hitch his horse to the log and snake it out to the haul road. Or for the butt log of a forest giant, they might use the go-devil, a small sled that went under the heavy end of a big log so it wouldn't plow snow. He saw how they muscled the small and middle-sized logs with cant hooks and picaroons and how the horses leaned into their harnesses when getting out the big logs.

Most exciting was watching the logs pile up on the double bobsled. A wide rack made of heavy oak timbers was mounted across the sled. Using horsepower and manpower, the sled tender gave the orders. The pile rose sometimes eight or more logs high.

"The record stands at thirty-two thousand board feet in a single load," Isaiah Green told them in the shanty one night. "The foreman says we're gonna go better than that this winter."

Sven didn't know how to figure board feet, but he determined he would learn. He'd ask Bates.

The amazing fact was that two horses could pull such a load of logs to the lakeshore. But each night a teamster with a water tank came down the skid road pouring water into the trenches cut by sled runners. The next morning, a smooth ice surface was ready to speed the sleds on the gentle slope to the unloading ramp.

"Hafta be sure the road don't get too steep," Bjarnie Syvertson explained while he and Sven watched a loaded sled pass on the skid road. "In one camp I worked, they spread hay on the road to slow down the sleds. Don't want a load like that to get moving faster than the horses can trot. You hafta think about stopping it where you want it."

In Sweden, young boys were often apprenticed by their parents to skilled tradesmen to learn a trade so they would have a way to earn a living when they became adults. And the Swedish trade master expected parents to pay him for educating their sons. Sven figured that here in this new land, the shanty boys were apprentice loggers, although they earned small wages.

Sven was putting on muscle and weight, and he had grown three inches since arriving at the Schmidt farm in August. He was grateful Papa had bought his clothes large enough to grow into. Even his boots, which had been so big he had to wear two pairs of socks so his feet didn't slip inside, were almost a perfect fit now. Like the other shanty boys, he wore the tops of his socks over his pants to prevent snow from packing up under the pant legs. If his pants were short, it didn't matter. His coat was growing tight across the shoulders. It couldn't be helped. Even if he had been willing to charge a new coat at the store, they didn't have one for a boy soon to turn thirteen. He had already checked that out.

CHAPTER 5

From Goodwill to Vengeance

Christmas was near. In the shanty even the roughest loggers began to talk about holidays they had spent with their families. They spoke about the good food their mothers and grandmothers had begun preparing weeks in advance. For the boys, talk of Christmas brought on a plague of homesickness that had to be smothered with wild outbreaks of fist fights. For Sven and Raf, their time in the barn offered unembarrassed honesty about their homeward yearnings.

"My mother is sending up a box of cookies," Raf confided to Sven one evening when they were both in the stable caring for the horses. "I had a letter from her yesterday when the new skidder came up. He's our neighbor. He stopped by our farm to tell my parents as he was leaving. Mama had no time to bake anything, but his son's starting as a bucker next week."

"Bill Sutherland says he knows how to make cookies, and he has butter and sugar and flour. He says that's all he needs." Sven passed on the young cookee's claims, remembering his disbelief. "It's the cardamom and anise and the shapes Mama makes with her tin cookie cutters," he said.

"And the almond paste and Mama's thumbprints," Raf agreed. "Dutch sweets won't taste like Swedish ones, but I'll share some with you."

"Better not," Sven warned his friend. "Every boy in the shanty will expect some if you do, and some of the loggers will too."

The next sled loads of supplies into McEllroy's Pinch River Camp also brought Christmas packages for all of the shanty boys except Arnie, Jamie, and Sven. The hand-knitted woolen socks, mittens, and caps, carefully wrapped small cookies and cakes reflected the traditions of each home. No shanty boy asked to sample Raf's Dutch cakes, not even the chocolate ones, for this would mean giving up one of his own cherished treats.

But Raf slipped two sugar crisps wrapped in white paper to Sven when Sven came to help him with the horses. Sven had hoped for a Christmas letter from Sweden, for he had written twice since arriving at the camp. Lesja knew how to address a letter. He had carefully copied the information from a letter Bates had received from his wife.

*   *   *   *   *

The French fiddler who had livened up the bunkhouse in the evenings through November had broken two fingers, and the hog boss's splints kept him from fiddling. They still had two harmonicas and a Jew's harp, but the loggers' boots on the plank floor drowned out the music. That and the clapping and singing. But the arrival of Christmas boxes put everyone in a festive mood. The fiddler made a spruce wreath and tied his red sash in a huge bow to decorate it. It hung from a nail on the edge of the bunk above his.

"Watch out for that nail," Arnie warned him.

He hadn't shut his mouth before the fiddler turned and caught his ear on the nailhead.

Loggers who lived on homesteads within twenty miles walked home for Christmas. Others spent the day around the stove in the shanty telling stories of tragedies and near tragedies they had witnessed, of the tallest trees and the biggest loads, the wildest river drives, the deepest snows. Sven lay on his top bunk where the warmth from the barrel stove hung like a damp blanket, for all along the edges of the top bunks damp socks and mittens were draped over clothesline ropes. Quiet as always, Papa sat on a bench near the fire listening to the stories and chuckling now and then.

Sven remembered Christmases in Stockholm when they had always been short of even the simplest food. Last year's Christmas had been filled with dreams of America. Papa had decided to leave Sweden to make a new start. Even then Papa had been very quiet, but he had been past changing his mind. Mama had been tearful. Little Karen had looked at Papa and then Mama and had hidden her head in Mama's apron. Sven remembered the long walk he and Lesja had taken through their shabby neighborhood, with its coal-dusted piles of shoveled snow and icy cobblestones.

"Once you've gone," Lesja had said, "you won't ever be able to come back. And if I go, it will be the same."

"We've never been back to the farm," Sven added in agreement. "That's the way things are. Things happen, and we can never go back to the way life used to be. I'll cut you a Christmas tree your first Christmas in America," he promised. "And boughs so you can weave a wreath."

"And we'll have butter again and sugar and eggs, and I'll make you *fattimand* and *Finska pinnar*."

* * * * *

After a huge Christmas feast in the cookhouse, Sven felt drowsy, and even with the noise and the thick tobacco smoke collecting in the space above his bunk, he dozed. He woke to angry shouts. Papa's voice rose, first in English, then switching to Swedish. Papa was swearing vehemently, and Sven had never heard such language coming from Papa's mouth.

Sven stretched to look down the row of bunks to the benches around the stove. Papa was on his feet, a handful of playing cards dropping from his grip. His body shook.

"You cheated me!" Papa roared. His fist balled suddenly, and his body spun behind his fist. He crashed full force into another man, and then they were both on the plank floor pounding each other while the other loggers just stepped back and watched.

After a short time, Papa and the other man both stood up and glared at each other. But neither of them said a word. Papa picked up the playing cards and handed them to still another man. He grabbed his mackinaw from the row of coats hanging on pegs beside the door and walked out, pulling the door shut behind him.

Sven felt more shaken than if he had been in on the beating. He watched gambling almost every night in the shanty. Every game someone lost money. Some won it back. Some never did. He could not believe that Papa had risked the money they had saved back for their future farm on a card game. Papa, who never took chances. Papa, who slept in his pants with their money in the inside pocket.

* * * * *

The French fiddler left Pinch River Camp soon after Christmas. He hadn't been playing in the shanty for a good while, but he had shouted and clapped his hands with the harmonica players, and he had sung loudly. Evenings in the shanty were less lively without the fiddler. And then one bitterly cold Saturday night, Sven came from grooming the horses in the barn to hear fiddle music rollicking across the snowdrifts again. Not one voice, but two fiddles rushing wildly through the tunes he already knew, and a new one just beginning as he reached the door.

Inside the shanty the lantern cast its brilliant light in four segments across the floor and the underside of the roof, where every clinched nail was white with frost. Through the bright squares of light into the muted glow and shadows, the loggers were dancing around the barrel stove, up and down the space between the bunks that lined both walls.

Isaiah Green was leaning against the bunk nearest the door. He winked at Sven and grabbed his arm. "Let's get Cookee," he said.

He nearly pushed Sven in front of him back out the door and across the path to the cookshack, where Bill Sutherland was still scrubbing up and the bull cook was spreading maple frosting on ten vast sheet cakes meant for Sunday dinner.

Sven was confused. This was forbidden territory.

"Got some aprons?" Isaiah hollered. "The new hands brought their fiddles."

To Sven's amazement, the bull cook let out a whoop and dropped his wide spatula. He dried his hands on his own apron then pulled out a wooden packing box in which his clean and folded aprons were stacked.

He handed an armful of aprons to Isaiah. "Deck the boys out and gear up the fiddlers. We'll be over to join in an hour." The cook handed Sven an armful of flour-sack dishtowels.

"Come on," Isaiah said.

When Isaiah opened the doors, the fiddlers stopped. There was a lot of loud talk, so fast Sven could not follow. In five minutes each of the shanty boys was rigged out with a skirt fashioned from two dish-towels with an apron over it all. Sven looked down at his own outfit in dismay. He was about to protest he would not play at being a girl when the fiddlers took up their fiddles, and Harrington grabbed his hand and spun him around and down the middle of the floor to the music. It was mostly loud, and Sven recognized the pattern the dance was taking, something like the street dances in the country villages in Sweden. Only here the boys wearing "skirts" were the "girls."

Sven was embarrassed. But the veteran shanty boys seemed to take the dress up as good fun. Isaiah wore an additional dishtowel tied around his head like an old woman's shawl. He sprang nimbly through the intricate dance with his apron strings flying.

The fiddlers rocked with their own music and called out to the dancers and to each other. The music went faster and faster, and the shanty shook with the logging boots pounding the plank floor. Finally, Sven found himself at the end of the shanty and climbed up to his own bunk and sat with his legs dangling, watching the show. Harmonica players joined in when one fiddler took a break for a dipperful of water from the bucket.

At last the door opened, and the bull cook entered, splendid in fresh white trousers, a long white shirt, and a tall white hat. Behind him came Bill Sutherland, dressed in white too, but as always, wearing his black bowler hat. The loggers stopped their dancing and roared.

"Here's for an Irish jig," shouted the bull cook.

The fiddlers looked at each other and said something Sven could not hear; then they dipped their shoulders toward each other and rocked back on their heels. Their bows sprang to the strings and the music erupted. The bull cook, though he was a thick-bodied man and usually moved around the cookshack with deliberation, began jigging, and then Isaiah Green dashed onto the floor to join him.

Their backs were as straight as the mast of a sailing ship, but their feet were fairly a blur, and they stepped high and sometimes kicked a leg out straight ahead. Sweat poured down the bull cook's face, and Isaiah's face grew red, but they jigged on until the fiddler gave out. The bull cook's white hat still stood firmly on his head.

"There's cake and ice cream in the cookshack," Bill Sutherland said.

The bull cook regained his dignity and walked ahead of the hundred men to the cookshack. Sven jumped down from his perch, took off the dishtowels and apron, folded them carefully, and draped them across his arm. Though it was cold outside, he did not put on a coat but rushed across the packed path to join the others.

They had all fallen silent at the cookshack door. Each man went directly to his own place at the table, and Bill Sutherland and the bull cook came with great bowls filled with ice cream. The foreman and Jamie brought the cut golden sheet cakes to each table. Each logger carefully lifted a piece of cake with his clean fork and waited for the ice cream bowl to come around.

They ate silently as always. When they were finished, the bull cook struck two pot covers together. "I want you boys to stay by and clean up."

The great tubs of hot water were waiting. Sven gathered up the tin plates while Raf gathered forks. Jamie was having a final piece of cake, and Bobby Cooper was scraping ice cream from a bowl. He grinned at Sven and turned toward the tub filled with soapy water. Bobby unbuttoned his shirt sleeves, rolled them up, and began washing tin plates as if he were swamping pine limbs ahead of a bucker. Sven rolled up his own sleeves and began fishing the plates from the hot water in the rinse tub. Others, with dishtowels in hand, grabbed them and dried them and reset the tables for Sunday breakfast.

Back in the shanty the loggers were sitting on their bunks or the benches pulled back around the stove. They were telling stories again about the biggest load of logs, the biggest log jam, the deepest snows. Sven saw Papa was playing cards again under the lantern.

Sven took off his boots, threw them up onto his bunk, then climbed up and stretched out.

Sunday morning the shanty smelled even stronger of whiskey than was usual for a Sunday morning. Sven put on his boots before dropping down from his bunk. Below him Papa was sound asleep, snoring lightly.

There had been no horn to awaken the loggers, this being their day off. Breakfast would be flapjacks as usual, but only for those who showed up in the cookshack.

The cows, however, must be milked on time, even on Sundays. Sven got the clean milk pail and strainer cloth as well as the shotgun can with its tight-fitting lid from Bill Sutherland. He set all his equipment, along with the lighted lantern, on the handsled and set out for the barn.

The world was totally silent except for the snow crunching beneath his boots. Wood smoke hovered in a luminous blanket over the cookshack roof and the roof of the shanty, its smell sweet with birch and maple.

Papa had been drinking the night before. This was the first time Sven had seen that happen, although for weeks Papa had been keeping company with men who drank too much and too often. They didn't sell whiskey at the company store, so Papa must be spending from their savings. Sven felt a deep ache settle behind his ribs. Papa seldom spoke to him anymore.

In the barn he hung the lantern on its peg and poured hot water from the shotgun can into the wash pan. He spoke to the cows in Swedish, wondering if Raf cajoled them in Dutch. With a clean cloth he washed the four udders and settled on the milk stool beside the first cow. He leaned his head into the Jersey's fawn-colored side. As his hands forced the milk from the teats in streams that rang in the bottom of the pail, he thought about Papa. What had happened to the Papa who had guarded his speech, who had guarded his money and his time, who liked to sit with the family around the table after a meal and listen to his children, to hold the baby?

* * * * *

Sunday passed as it always did at the Pinch River Camp with loggers banding together in groups of three or four to boil their dirty cotton underclothes in one of the several half barrels set over outdoor fires. The washed clothing, still a dull gray, was wrung out and hung on clotheslines outside to freeze, then brought into the shanty to finish drying. A few woolen long-handles, socks, and mittens were washed in cold water every night of the week, and the shanty always smelled of rank, wet wool. The black or gray woolen trousers would go unwashed all winter, along with blankets and quilts.

Sven and Raf and the teamsters were the only residents of the shanty who worked on Sundays. The milk cows must be milked. The barn must be cleaned. The livestock must be fed and clean beds spread for them. The bull cook and Bill Sutherland worked harder on Sundays than on any other day, for loggers expected the noon meal to rise to regal grandeur.

Sven reflected after his breakfast of flapjacks that the cake they had eaten the night before had been planned for Sunday dinner.

They could hardly expect anything more than dried fruit pies for dessert today. He was right. There were apple and raisin and prune pies. Good, but only everyday fare.

While they were in the cookshack eating Sunday dinner, snow began to fall with flakes half the size of birch leaves fluttering in a light wind. When the men in the shanty settled back into their usual Sunday afternoon laundry detail, the boys pulled on their coats and went outside for a snowball fight. They divided up into teams, with Arnie rallying one group and Isaiah Green leading the other.

Bobby Cooper pulled an aspen pole from the woodpile and placed it across the sled road.

"That's the boundary," he said. "When one side gives ground, the other side moves over the line. If the whole invading team makes it across the line, the battle's won."

"We'll have as many battles as we can before it starts getting dark," Arnie said. "Come on, men. Make your snowballs."

Isaiah had a different plan. He called his team around him. "Everybody make ten snowballs, then five of you keep on making snowballs while the others attack Arnie and his men. We'll surprise them." Isaiah counted off his team members. "Evens lead the attack. Odds keep packing snowballs."

Sven was relieved that he was number seven. He might get hit by a few stray snowballs. But though he would never have said so, his arms were tired from pitching wet straw and manure most of the morning while the others had sat around yarning or stirring their clothes in the wash barrels.

He settled himself just behind the low wall of snow thrown back time after time by the horse-drawn snowplow and began packing fistfuls of snow. He packed more loose snow around the small ball, then set each finished missile along the top of the snowbank.

"There, Noodge," he called. "Use some of mine."

Isaiah suddenly gave the signal, and half his team rushed toward enemy territory, each with his left arm clutched to his middle with an armful of snowballs.

Sven looked up to watch the first few hits, then concentrated on making more snowballs as rapidly as he could. Noodge came back and scooped up a new supply of ammunition, followed by Giles Andrews, a shanty boy new since Christmas.

"Good work, Sven," Giles said. "I'll be back."

Sven had friends on both sides, Jamie and Raf with the enemy. But he was working for Isaiah Green and his own team. He was almost disappointed when Isaiah and his teammates yelled their victory when the battle had hardly begun.

"No fair!" Arnie shouted angrily. "You were supposed to give us time to build up our supply."

"Who said that?" Bobby asked, grinning. "Nobody said anything about that rule before we started."

"Well, everybody knows that's how it's supposed to be done," Arnie blustered.

"A good general surprises the enemy," Bobby said. "Didn't you learn about that in history class?"

"School?" Arnie snorted. "Never been there. What's school got to do with making a living?"

"Isaiah's been to school," Bobby said. "You can be a soldier without going to school, but you'll never be a general without an education."

"This isn't the army!" Arnie snapped.

"Shut your mouth, Arnie," Jamie said. "Let's play another round. I lead this one."

Sullenly, Arnie set to making snowballs fifty feet down the sled road from Sven. Even at that distance, Sven could see Arnie grab chunks of ice where water had sloshed over the rim of the water barrels when Bates iced the runner tracks.

"Watch out for Arnie's snowballs," Sven warned Bobby Cooper. He nodded toward Arnie, who was bent over his pile. Bobby saw the ice going into the snowballs and passed the word down the line.

Just as Sven guessed, Arnie did not share his supply with another player. He gathered up all of them in his coat front and charged toward the boundary when Isaiah's team started firing. To Arnie's surprise, the whole opposing team closed in on him, knocking him off balance as he ducked first one direction and then another between flying snowballs.

Sven kept packing handfuls of snow, but he laughed as he watched Arnie finally drop his left arm and run. The loaded snowballs rolled along the road, and Isaiah's team grabbed them up as they rushed after Arnie, pelting him with his own weapons. That single-minded pursuit cost Isaiah's team that round, but it was a loss they all enjoyed.

After the sixth round, with each team winning three, they brushed the snow from their pants and coats and shook out their hats. Inside the shanty they crowded around the barrel stove between the washtubs and sagging clotheslines.

"Do you want me to help you with your chores?" Sven asked Raf.

Raf nodded. While he was pouring hot water into the clean milk pails, Sven got the strainer cloths. "Get a mixing spoon and a flat skimming pan," Raf told him.

They set off up the road to the barns. "What's this stuff for?" Sven asked, tucking the spoon and pan under his arm so his hands were free to carry the lantern.

Raf leaned against the rope pulling the handsled up the slope. "Did you see how Bill Sutherland made the ice cream?"

"He said he set a tin dishpan filled with custard in a pan of crushed ice and rock salt and just kept stirring it until it froze," Sven said.

"My mother lets us make snow cream," Raf said. "It's faster and easier. I got a cupful of sugar from the barrel. It's in a brown paper bag in my pocket. Scoop up a panful of clean snow while it's light enough to make sure it's fresh-fallen and set it up on the haystack 'til we finish milking."

Sven fed the four cows while Raf began milking the first Jersey. When he finished the first cow, Raf strained the milk into the tall shotgun can and put on its lid. Then before he sat down by the second Jersey, Raf put the shotgun can outside in a snowbank.

"We want it cold," he said.

Sven had by this time nearly finished the black and white Friesian. He put the strainer cloth on the second tall can and poured in his milk, then settled beside the red cow with the white "paint" on her face.

He watched Raf set down his milk pail, and through the open door watched Raf pour off some of the cooled milk into the skimming pan before straining the last of his milk into the can of cooled milk. Raf then took up the spoon and began stirring the milk and snow vigorously.

"Come along," Raf said. "The snow cream is almost ready."

Sven drew the last few weak squirts of milk from the cow's teats before standing up.

Five minutes later they were seated outside the barn on the bank of snow thrown back when the doorway was shoveled out. The lantern light shone upon the snow at their feet and upon the panful of snow beaten to smoothness with rich Jersey top milk. Sven felt the cold rising up through the seat of his pants into his hips and spreading down his legs. He felt the cold wind dashing new snow against his face and the cold numbing the roof of his mouth, the cold sweetening on his tongue and oozing down his throat so nearly frozen he could hardly swallow it.

"It's good," he said.

"I knew you'd like it," Raf said. "Mama lets us make it at home whenever there's a clean, fresh snow."

They passed the one spoon back and forth between them until they finally finished the whole skimming panful. Sven's belly felt like he was filled with solid ice. His whole body ached from the cold. But he licked the spoon when they were done and set the milk cans and pails onto the handsled. He pulled the load down the hill, breaking its speed with his leg when the sled gained speed. Raf walked behind him with the lantern, whose light glittered on the white sled road and on the falling snowflakes.

* * * * *

Monday morning when the hog boss sounded wake-up, Sven waited for someone to light the lantern over the barrel stove. Down through the middle of the shanty two dozen pairs of long-handles sprang like headless man-sized puppets when Bates came down off his top bunk and caught the clothesline rope with his shoulder.

Bobby Cooper laughed, then reached out and gave the rope a deliberate tug.

"Hop lively, lads," he said.

"I had just started sleeping," Arnie complained. "This place smells like a sheep pen after a heavy rain."

"It smells better than it would if nobody washed socks and underwear 'til spring," Noodge McUftee said. He was sitting on the edge of his bunk with one boot on and laced and the other in his hands.

Bobby Cooper dropped to the floor. He grabbed Noodge's bootless foot and sniffed. "Them clean socks?"

"I washed mine last week. Can't you still smell the lye soap?" Noodge pulled on his second boot and laced it swiftly.

Sven had learned that since his bunk was farthest from the door, he might as well plan to be the last out of the shanty. He finally reached for his heavy woolen trousers, threw back his covers, and pulled them on. He felt glad that he had carried an extra bucket of hot water to the barn the day before and had a "soap and pour" bath before changing into his clean long-handles.

At noon Sven climbed onto the sled with Bill Sutherland and the huge kettles of food. When they reached the cuttings, he helped Bill pull down the plank tailgate, which served as a table for serving out the bowls of hot bean soup. He took one handle of the nearest pot and helped Bill maneuver it back, then handed Bill the tin dipper and pushed the box of tin bowls where the cookee could reach them. Once the big pan of double-stacked corn bread was where the loggers could take a piece in passing, Sven took over the coffee pot. He'd had his own meal in the warm cookshack. Now it was his job to see the hundred men fed as quickly as possible. Daylight was precious in January.

When Bill Sutherland had everything stowed a half hour later, Sven took up his ax and followed the hog boss. The foreman signaled him to follow a big Swede with a red-gold mustache that concealed his lips. Sven could see the Swede was in ill humor. He could hear him muttering threats in Swedish that included the hog boss, the buckers, and the swampers. In a final outburst, he added curses on the teamsters and the cooks before returning to call down even more dire luck on the foreman.

Sven wondered what had happened during the morning to bring on this rage. He determined to stay out of that man's reach and to work so fast the Swede would have no call to turn around and look back.

The first tree came down with a crash. Sven jumped in with his ax, slashing off the top and the small limbs near it before moving down the trunk to the butt of the huge log. He stepped up on it and jumped down on the other side. He raised his ax and swung hard into the bottom limb.

"TIMBER!" yelled the Swede.

Sven saw Arnie leaping from the sidelines to begin swamping the limbs on that pine.

"There, boy, give me your ax," the Swede told Arnie.

Sven noticed the birch sapling close by the next pine the Swedish feller planned to cut.

"Where's your own ax?" Arnie snapped. He set to slashing limbs, but the Swede came back and took hold of his arm. Instead of giving over to the big man, Arnie began swearing. He kicked the man in the shins and took a swing at his middle. The feller knocked him down with a single swat then kicked him in the ribs. He took the ax and sliced off the birch sapling. He then set the ax headfirst into the snow beside Arnie, who by this time was back on his feet, though doubled in pain, holding his side.

Sven stood for only a moment before returning to his swamping.

Arnie was back at work and finished limbing his log before the Swede called "TIMBER" again.

Sven felt sorry for Arnie in spite of the feelings of anger that had often risen inside him when Arnie boasted or bluffed or got violent with the other boys. Sven had himself been the object of Arnie's anger more than once. But he had been close enough to hear the dull thud of the logger's boot against the other boy's body.

That night in the shanty Sven woke twice hearing Arnie's muffled groans. But the next day Arnie was at breakfast and headed out of camp carrying his ax when the loggers set off for the cuttings.

"I'm worried about the boy," Bates told Sven in the barn while he was rubbing down his team that evening before supper. "Not that he didn't have it coming, but a grown man has no business abusing a kid that way, no matter what he's done."

"Arnie has no manners," Sven said.

Bates laughed. "We don't call good behavior *manners* here," Bates said. "But *respect* is another matter. If a boy don't learn to respect those above him when he's young, he won't get far in life. I guess the sooner that boy learns some respect, the better."

"He's hurting pretty bad," Sven said.

"By the time he's done hurting, he'll be wiser," Bates said. He forked his team a mangerful of hay then walked with Sven back to the cookshack, where Bill Sutherland was just coming out with the short horn.

* * * * *

Before the end of the next day, Arnie was coughing in the woods. That night he coughed, but he did not cry out, though Sven knew he must be in terrible pain, for certainly he had broken ribs. Bates was hitching up his team when Sven reached the barn at four thirty the next morning.

"I'm taking that boy in to Grand Rapids," he said. "He's in no shape to work, and we've no nursemaid more tender than the hog boss."

Sven knew Arnie had no one in Grand Rapids. He wondered what would become of the boy.

When Bates returned the following day, he brought the mail, which included a letter from Sam Duell and Bobby Cooper's mother. Her husband had broken a leg in a fall. He'd been shoveling the snow from the roof in fear that the accumulating weight would break down the roof. Their mother asked the boys to come home to Battle Creek to do the farm chores. They settled at the office then set off before noon. Sven hated to see them go. Three of the original shanty boys gone in three days.

Papa had begun building a timber platform near the iced-over river. Sven examined it in the half light, walking back to the barn after breakfast one morning. He could see it was meant to float and guessed it must have something to do with the log drive in the spring.

"It's a wanigan," Harrington told him when he asked. "It's a big one. The river boss must plan for the men to sleep on it."

"Papa will build a little house on it?" Sven spread a forkful of clean straw then went for more. He guessed it would be more like a small cookshack with bunks.

"This spring's drive should involve thirty, maybe forty men," Harrington said as he finished currying a second team and moved on to the third stall. "The company has three shacks on high ground between here and the Grand. Some of the drivers will bed down in them. The crew will be spread down the river for thirty miles. You'll see."

From Lemon Pie
to Further Violence

It was early February.

Arnie, looking thinner than usual but some improved, was with Bates when he returned from his next trip to Grand Rapids. In the bobsled loaded with supplies was a commodity that surprised even the bull cook. The Irishman sprang around the kitchen and fairly jigged.

"Lemons!" he shouted. "A bushel of lemons! What absolute wealth! Pure gold! Pies we shall have, with meringue as light as clouds floating over lemon custard so smooth we'll dream of paradise!"

Sven grinned at Bill Sutherland, who was lugging a third fifty-pound bag of sugar to the barrel beside the bull cook's worktable. Bill pulled the cotton string with practiced hand, and the entire top of the cloth sack opened. Bill poured the sugar into the barrel. "He'll let me roll out the pie crusts and bake them. And he'll let me whip the egg whites for the meringue."

Sven remembered the lemon pie Mrs. Schmidt had made the summer before in Indiana. He imagined thirty lemon pies set in a row along the bull cook's table and Bill Sutherland cutting each into fourths.

"Here's the rest of your eggs," Bates told the bull cook, setting down a double wooden crate with heavy paper dividers separating the eggs. "Six crates instead of nine. Hens are falling behind on their laying this late in the winter. The poultry man claims they'll pick up again as soon as the weather breaks."

"And when the weather breaks, we'll be breaking camp," the bull cook scoffed. "Well, we shall have lemon pies and never spare the eggs, though we have bacon without eggs for the rest of the month."

Sven knew Bates had wrapped the egg crates in woolen quilts and stacked bags of flour and sugar and tubs of lard around them to keep them from freezing on the twenty-mile drive.

"Lemon pies we shall have," Bill Sutherland said as Sven poured boiling water into a shotgun can and took the milk pails from their place under the table. "With golden, creamy custard and towering meringue. That means four eggs for each pie by my calculations."

"One hundred and twenty?" Sven could hardly believe that nearly half a crate of eggs would go into the pies. And yet, that was about one egg for each lumberman, not as many as if Bill fried them on the big griddle for breakfast.

He carried his equipment to the handsled and loaded up.

Bates handed him a letter. "No need to pass it through the hog boss, Sven. No reason you should wait another day to get it."

Sven saw the nearly transparent paper and knew at once the message was from Lesja. He tucked the envelope into his coat pocket and stepped into the rope loop to pull the sled uphill to the barn, where he would join Raf doing evening chores.

Sven felt intense pride now, as he always did, that he and his friend were in charge of the milk and cream and even the butter for the whole Pinch River Camp. Ten gallons of milk each morning and ten gallons more each evening. The milking, the cooling, the skimming, the churning.

Halfway up the hill, Sven stopped to rest. He took the letter from his pocket and removed his right mitten. With his thumbnail, he slit the envelope, and then he pulled out the double-folded sheet of paper. He still had trouble reading even simple words in English, but Lesja's letter was simple—in Swedish.

Dear Brother,

I have nothing but sad news. Mama is taken sick again, the second time since you and Papa left us. Baby Peter is not well, but I am determined to make him strong again if I can buy him milk again soon. He is trying to walk about the kitchen now, but his legs are weak, and the bones bow out as if he had been on horseback from the day he was born. Karen has been sick, too, but I am well as I always am. I rejoice that you and Papa are well fed, though you work so very hard in the cold forest. I pray each day that God will bring us all together again, though sometimes I fear it can never be. We are seeking a place where we can live with a family and work for our keep, since we can no longer live in Grandpa Oldstrom's place. We try not to grieve, but I am sad, and I cannot deny that I am. I am lonesome for you, Sven, and for Papa. I can almost hear his voice in the old kitchen, calling us all to come to table in his gentle way. Give Papa a kiss for me and one for Karen and one for Peter. Mama sends her love.

Your sister, Lesja

Tears welled in Sven's eyes. What had happened to Grandpa Oldstrom? Why were they to be put out of his house? He put the letter back in his pocket and went on to the barn. He did not tell Papa of the letter. He did not even tell Raf, though Raf had talked with Arnie and had news to pass along.

"Bobby was right. Arnie's folks is all dead. He's always bragging on his pa, but he's got nobody. Bates has a brother in Grand Rapids. He left Arnie for his brother's wife to take care of. Arnie's down a notch, but he's glad to be back to work."

* * * * *

Only a few days later Isaiah Green came from the cuttings with lips swollen horribly. When he opened his mouth to speak, Sven saw a gaping space where his upper teeth should have been.

69

Sven wanted to stare at Isaiah's bloodied mouth, but he looked away.

"He didn't pick the fight," Noodge McUftee told Sven and Raf outside the cookshack. "It was that same ruffian Swede that kicked Arnie in the ribs. He got Isaiah across the mouth with an ax handle and knocked his teeth flying like wood chips. The foreman called the Swede on it. He owed more than he had coming at the store, but he's gone packing. We're all of us glad. He never laid for the men—just us boys."

Sven was relieved that the hog boss had assigned Arnie to help the axman by knocking loose broken ax handles and replacing them in the shop.

The same week two other loggers drifted off, and four new men hired on. The men who came seemed to Sven about the same kind as those who left, shabby and restless and ready to stay long enough to charge a new outfit at the store and get a few weeks of better than average food. Even with the violent Swede gone, Sven and the other boys watched their step, never got in the way of a feller or a bucker, and never answered back out of turn. Bill Sutherland was the only man without a beard to speak up boldly to the logging crew. He didn't need to tell the other boys it was because he was destined to be a full cook on the log drive in April and May.

Sven watched Isaiah Green come to meals with his lips so stiff he could hardly open them. The bull cook brought him broth and coddled eggs and oatmeal gruel to keep up his strength, for Isaiah was determined to stay on and finish the season on Pinch River.

"He'll make the drive too," Raf said a few days after the attack. Raf stopped beside the haystack and looked up at Sven. "Isaiah's Irish and he's tough."

Sven was brushing snow from the top of an untouched haystack. He drove his fork deep into the layer of coarse slough grass that topped the stack. He threw it down for bedding the animals. Then he pulled several forkfuls of dry meadow hay down and started carrying it into the barn.

Raf took another forkful and followed him.

"Someday Isaiah will meet up with that Swede, and he'll even the score. That Swede will lose more than his front teeth. I'd head for Oregon if I were that Swede."

"He had better watch out for me too," Sven said. He remembered the snowball fight and how intelligently Isaiah had managed the whole game, as if it had been a real battle. Bobby Cooper had said Isaiah was a good general because he'd been to school. Sven wondered what dreams Isaiah had for his future. For certain, his handsome smile was gone forever. If Isaiah had planned to be a doctor or a lawyer or a businessman, he had better kiss those dreams goodbye. People never trusted a man with missing or broken front teeth.

"Wonder if he's got a sweetheart back home," Raf said as he spread his hay for two of the cows.

Harrington had been listening to the conversation while he unharnessed his team outside the barn. He turned from hanging the harness on its peg on the log wall to look squarely at Sven.

"You still planning on that farm?" Harrington asked. "You and your dad?"

"I'm planning," Sven said, though he felt less certain now each day that it would happen.

"You can see for yourself where logging gets a man," Harrington said. "If you want a farm, hire on helping a farmer and learn all you can before you turn twenty-one. Save your earnings, and go West and claim yourself a homestead. You may be hard put to find a farmer who will treat you like family, but even the worst won't beat up on you."

"Everyone's been good to me here," Sven said. "And the food's good."

"Isaiah Green was better looking than he ought to have been," Harrington conceded. "He was as good a swamper as they come and a fair bucker too. He swaggered a little, and a lot of the big men with crooked noses, and noses and chins turned red from frostbite and whiskey, take pleasure in smashing a handsome face. Logging's a dangerous life no matter how you look at it. Don't do this another season, boys. Find yourselves safer jobs."

"Bjarnie Syvertson's father was killed in a flour mill last winter," Raf said. "In an explosion."

Harrington patted the rump of the black Clydesdale on his right. "And you could get kicked by a horse working for a farmer in Iowa as soon as in the barn here. It's the truth. But logging is dangerous work, and it draws dangerous men. And men who come in steady and decent are just as likely to leave drunkards and destitute."

"I'm working three logging seasons," Raf said. "My parents don't have enough work on our farm for as many children as they've got. My brother came out all right. I'll be all right too. I'm not handsome like Isaiah was, and I don't swagger none. I'm special careful not to swagger. We were warned."

Harrington smiled, but his smile faded. "Raf, you have a home you can walk to if you need to leave camp. Sven, you can't go back to your people in Sweden if things go badly. You'll have to take care that things turn out right. This isn't the place for a boy six years from manhood."

Sven did not correct Harrington. He had not yet had a birthday. He was not yet thirteen. If twenty-one marked the beginning of manhood, that was a long way off.

He wanted to tell Harrington about Mama's sickness and little Peter's crooked legs and Karen's cough, but that would seem disloyal to Papa. Harrington knew Papa wouldn't have money to send for Mama and the children after a second year of logging. He didn't say so, but he knew. And Sven knew it most certainly.

That night in his bunk he lay awake thinking about Lesja's letter. *What if Mama dies? What if Peter grows up crippled? What if they all die hungry while Papa and I eat pie three times a day and have all the milk and butter we want, and biscuits and cornbread and flapjacks and beans and meat?* Papa slept soundly in the bunk below him with no signs of bad dreams or even fears. Across the way and down three bunks, Isaiah Green was having trouble breathing. His nose had been smashed as well as his teeth. There was no helping it. He had to breathe through an open mouth, with air drying the bruised tissues. When Isaiah worked outdoors, the cold passed over the raw nerves of his broken teeth.

Winter days were milder now with February almost past, and even the nights were less intensely cold. During the afternoons, icicles dripped along the south edges of all the camp roofs. The ice roads in deep shade were still solidly frozen in midafternoon, but on the sunny slope up to the barns, the tracks were softening. The deep snow banks had settled under warm skies, though the temperature seldom rose above freezing.

"One month more before the roads break up," the hog boss announced in the cookshack one evening after supper. "I want all the good pine on the riverbank or on skids on the lakeshore before we shut down." He mentioned the sections finished and the ones where timber still stood.

In the stories around the barrel stove in the shanty that night, the sleds were loaded higher, the loggers themselves were more powerful than usual. There was a great deal of shouting and challenging. Then the fiddlers brought out their fiddles, someone started jigging, and the whole crew sang or shouted with the music.

Two days later they were all kept indoors with a blizzard that left two feet of new snow. It was light as goose down and floated before a brisk wind into drifts that blocked windows and doors and filled the plowed logging roads.

Sven and Raf had their barn chores to do, and several of the teamsters made use of their time repairing harnesses and currying and brushing their teams. The blacksmith replaced worn horseshoes. Every ax in camp was sharpened on the grindstone in the shop.

Sven joined the other shanty boys there, out of the storm, taking turns treadling the grindstone beside a fire. Here they were a bit more to themselves than in the shanty with the one hundred adult loggers, nearly all of the men smoking, some of them drinking, and some of them getting touchy over losses from playing cards.

Arnie had heard about Isaiah's encounter with the same big Swede who had broken his ribs. He ran his thumb and forefinger around the ax handle he had just smoothed with a rasp.

"There's two of us laying for that man," Arnie muttered to the boys on the bench beside the shop stove. "I'll be a man grown before I get a chance, but I won't forget his face or the shape of his back. I just hope I see his back before I see his face. I won't wait for him to turn around." It was a long day, too soon after Sunday to wash clothes.

"What about a snowball fight?" Jamie suggested.

There was a general protest.

"And lose our one day off to rest all winter?"

"There's too much wind."

"It's too cold."

Sven knew they were just too tired. Besides, with Arnie still sore in the middle and Isaiah guarding his mouth and nose, they could hardly muster two teams.

Sven shambled through knee-deep snow to the cookshack and spoke quickly with Bill Sutherland. He came back with his news.

"We'll make snow cream." He beat a tattoo on the cook's largest tin washpan with an enormous spoon. "Raf, there's a gallon of top milk in the shotgun can outside. Here's the sugar. I'll fill the pan with clean snow."

Though others were willing to beat the snow cream, Raf would have none of it. It was his recipe, and he would do the honors. Sven presumed upon Bill Sutherland for enough spoons to go around. All the shanty boys knelt around the pan on the shop floor, shuddering when the cold drove up through the roofs of their mouths and pierced their brains, rubbing between their eyes to relieve the sharp stab of pain, then scooping up another mouthful. The dim afternoon light passed through a few inches of glass not buried in the drift outside the shop. Sven and Raf enlisted Jamie to help them get the milking equipment through the drifts up to the barn and the milk back.

That night the wind drove a fine dust of snow through cracks around the windows and even under the eaves across the foot of

Sven's bed. He covered his head with the corner of his blanket and slept, but in his dreams he heard Mama crying, and he awoke certain that little Peter had died. If it were really so, he remembered, he and Papa would not get the news for at least six weeks. Heartsick, trying to force himself to believe that the dream had come only because of the wild cries of the wind, he pulled on his boots and laced them up. It was morning, he was certain, although the hog boss had not shouted them out of bed. Sven had his chores.

The snowfall continued through the morning, adding still another eight inches to the twenty-four that had fallen on the first day of the storm. When the sky cleared in midafternoon, loggers came out with shovels to dig out doorways and windows and to locate sleds. Teamsters and skidders all hitched up their horses to makeshift plows contrived with planks and chains. Before dark the sled roads were clear up the hillside to the barns, along Pinch River to the cuttings, and up the shallow draw to the eighty acres of good pine not yet started.

Bates and Harrington had loaded twenty barrels on each of their sleds, and the loggers had chopped a hole in the river's ice and hauled water to fill the barrels. Now the teamsters set out down the two roads on which the logs would be hauled in the morning, two men on the back of each sled poured water in the tracks behind the runners. Behind Bates and behind Harrington followed another team pulling a sled to cut deeper tracks in the freezing slush.

Sven and Raf watched for a few minutes then pulled their hand-sled with the shotgun cans half full of hot water and the milk pails up the hill to the barn.

After a supper of stewed beef with rutabagas and potatoes and onions and great chunks of cornbread, the hog boss got up to make a speech.

"We've missed two days of work with this snowstorm," he said. But he looked pleased. "It's possible, if the weather doesn't warm up too fast, that we'll have another full month of good sledding. We can't count on it, but it looks better. We can't slack off in getting the timber out, but what's eighty acres to a hundred men, all well fed and in prime condition? Keep moving forward as fast as you can, but let's not get anybody else killed."

"First time I ever heard one of the big men worry about getting us out alive," Arnie commented as the boys settled in their own corner of the shanty, listening to the fiddlers and the harmonica players.

The musicians ran through some Polish tunes and then a Swedish folk dance before taking up an Irish jig. Sven glanced at Isaiah Green. Isaiah's eyes did not come up from the floor between his feet. His toes did not so much as tap to the music. Sven wondered what was going on inside Isaiah's head, but the other boy's face was impossible to read. His nose was only a bit crooked. His lips were no longer swollen. But his upper lip sagged against a jawbone where teeth ought to fill it out. The music gathered speed, and Sven felt almost like a top spinning to the sound. Isaiah's lower jaw stiffened, and he swallowed. His back stiffened, and he got up and walked down the middle of the shanty to the door on the far end.

The music had ended and the lanterns had been blown out when Sven heard Isaiah return to his bunk. He heard Isaiah's boots drop to the planks at the foot of his bed. After a while, he heard the other boy's loud breathing, for even with his nose healed, he could breathe only through his open mouth.

* * * * *

Bates was making one more trip to Grand Rapids for supplies since the superintendent expected to keep the operation going another month.

"They can spare Raf altogether in the woods while we're gone," he said. "The hog boss said I could have you to drive the second team, Sven. And Raf can do your share of the barn chores."

Sven welcomed the trip out to town, for he, like most of the other shanty boys, had not been out of the Pinch River Camp since early November when they had brought in winter supplies in wagons with the milk cows tied behind.

CHAPTER 7

From Milk Pail
to Roast Beef

The drive to Grand Rapids was mostly long and tiresome for Sven. He was alone on the big bobsled, his horses plodding along the forest sled road through heavy, unpacked snow. They passed through cutover land as well as mixed forest not considered useful to a logging company interested only in white pine. They stopped at dark in a log cabin no bigger than the sled itself with a lean-to shed where Bates sheltered the two teams. The teamster took two Hudson's Bay blankets from the sled after they fed the horses.

"Can't leave blankets here. Rats or squirrels get into them."

Sven took the lantern Bates handed him. Inside the cabin he lit the lamp and looked around.

"Built it myself," Bates said as he laid a fire in the potbellied stove. There was a mangerlike bunk on either side with hay for a bed. "It's not much, but it sure beats sleeping under canvas on winter trips. I figure next winter I'll be hauling another full day's drive up Pinch River to the new camp. When we break up the buildings in April, they'll leave me the harness room and part of the barn for a stopping-off place."

"What about the cows?" Sven asked.

"Oh, they'll make some good beef. Can't bother with leading them back out to sell, and sure can't keep them all summer in pasture with no fences."

Sven said nothing. Beef on the table along with the beans and biscuits was one thing. Beef that the same week had been a fawn-colored Jersey cow with a white rim around her black muzzle, who sometimes licked his sleeve or switched him with her black-tipped tail—that was an entirely different matter.

Bates said they would spend the next night in Grand Rapids at his brother's home.

"He sells shoes," Bates said. "Has a store just up from the railroad bridge, but he lives farther out on twenty acres. We can put up the horses, but his wife won't let us sleep in the house."

"Lice?" Sven guessed.

Bates nodded. "Once I brought in lice. She claimed they just took up residence—immigrated while I was sleeping. I always believed they would have been all right if she hadn't made me take a bath while she boiled my clothes." Bates winked. "When I got down into that tub of hot water with the lye soap, they had nothing to do but abandon me."

Sven laughed. In camp boiling his clothes had helped, and his secret soap and pour baths in the barn had helped too, but after sleeping in his bunk he always found himself scratching again within a day or two.

Bates talked about the log drive while he melted snow on the stove. "When that's over," he said, "I'll go back to hauling with company wagons for the summer. Once the roads dry out, I'll take the lumber from this year's camp up to the next location."

"Mr. Harrington has a farm," Sven commented.

"I never did," Bates said. "I like horses, and even cows in moderation, but I don't hanker for fields and planting and harvesting. Cutting hay is about as bad as things get for me." The teamster fixed tea with part of the hot water, and while it cooled, washed his face with a dingy cloth he plucked from a nail in the wall behind the stove.

"I want a farm," Sven said.

He told Bates about Grandfather Anderson's farm in Sweden, about having to leave it when Uncle Jens came back from the army.

"Papa did all the work keeping everything for him while he was away, but Uncle Jens was older, so he got it. Grandfather said that was the way it should be. But Papa built the new cattle barn and a granary. Papa thought Uncle Jens would stay in the army."

"Or die in the war and never come home," Bates guessed. He handed Sven a tin cup and sipped his own tea. "It was a gamble. Some soldiers live to come back from war. You can't count on them dying."

"Were you ever a soldier?" Sven lifted the packed hay in his bunk and shook it out. He sat down to take off his boots.

Bates said nothing. His back was turned, so Sven could not read his face, but after hesitating a long time, the teamster said, "I was at Gettysburg."

"Gettysburg?" Sven stretched out on the lumpy straw and flipped the blanket over the knees of his woodsman's trousers and feet in his woolen socks. He wiggled his toes until the blanket covered them.

"I guess just coming from Sweden you don't know about the Civil War," Bates said. Sven didn't answer, but he could tell this wasn't a time to ask questions.

"Life's uncertain whichever way you look at it," Bates said. He turned out the lantern and climbed into his bunk on the opposite wall. The bunks were so close in the narrow cabin that Sven could hear the teamster catch his breath twice before he went on. "I lost a lot of good friends in the war—more to sickness than to wounds. War's a dangerous game. But logging is a worse dangerous thing. Every day's a battle, and the enemy is just as often your friend who just isn't thinking sharp enough at the moment. I'm too old to walk into the woods every day wondering if I'm going to die. I'll die for sure someday, but not likely under a load of logs or a falling white pine."

Sven thought about that for a while before commenting. "Jamie says there's no use in saving up to buy a farm. His father and his grandfather died young logging."

"Jamie's right," Bates said. "If you plan to stick with logging, you'll likely die young. I most particular asked the hog boss to let you and Raf do the barn chores most of the time. At least you're out of harm's way half of each day. Raf's dad is a friend of my brother's. I told him I'd look out for the boy."

"Do you have boys of your own?" Sven asked.

"Two," Bates said. "They both went to California to the big timber. I haven't heard from them in a good while."

Bates said no more, and Sven was silent too. He wondered if Bates worried about his sons in the big timber in faraway California. Bates never talked about a wife, so his wife must be dead. That meant that like Jamie, Bates had no home except one logging camp after another. Some things about life in the camp were exciting, but Bates and Harrington were right about the dangers. Sven wasn't certain that the excitement made the danger acceptable. He thought about Isaiah Green's crooked nose and missing teeth and Arnie's broken ribs. He didn't have seven or eight years to make up his mind whether he wanted to be a real logger. There was plenty of danger for a boy of thirteen.

*   *   *   *   *

The following day they got to town in time to buy supplies and load the two wagons. When this was done, they drove to the edge of Grand Rapids, where Bates's brother made his home. Just as the teamster had predicted, his sister-in-law met them on the back porch with a kettle of hot water and a bar of soap that smelled like turpentine.

"This won't last," Sven said. "But it will feel good to sleep one night without scratching lice."

"That concoction's great for killing parent and child among them. Better start with your hair," Bates advised when they were stripped to the waist in the washhouse with gallons of sudsy water in two wash tubs. "Work up a good lather. Dunk your head in the tub real quick, then slap the lather on and rub it in."

With a generous bath and clean clothes followed by his first family meal since leaving the Schmidt farm in October, Sven felt like a king. Bates's brother and his wife were grandparents, they said, and after supper they took him into their small parlor and showed him photographs of their daughter's family, including two boys taller than their father, a girl in braids, and two small boys leaning against their mother.

"Mama and my sister Lesja and the little ones didn't come over with us," Sven told them. He explained about the farm he and Papa would buy after saving their money and tried to sound as if he still believed in the dream, though it was fading fast. He looked at the pleasant room with its organ with red velvet behind carved leaves and vines, its round table with a family Bible and a milk-white lamp set in the middle of a spotless white linen tablecloth, its two brocade-covered chairs and sleek black settee. A woman had given him a small paper-covered Bible in Stockholm, and he and Lesja had read it sometimes to Mama, who loved its comforting words but could not read it herself. Sven's throat tightened.

Mrs. Bates smiled and put an arm around his shoulders. "Everyone who comes to America comes with a dream. It's always hard for the newcomers. It will be hard for you and your father. But all of us who have made a place for ourselves had to start somewhere. We were lucky, for our grandparents came over from England a great while ago and left us better off than they were at first. We hope to pass on a better life for our children's children. You'll have to be braver than our grandsons, but they will have to work themselves, for their father cannot just break up his farm among them all and pass it on. They each will need a full one hundred sixty acres if they want to provide well for their own families."

"They'll go West for free land," her husband said.

"Our son will take over the store," Mrs. Bates said. "But his sons will go West as well. Ever since the first settlers from Europe settled along the Atlantic coast, the young men with ambition have ventured to the west of settlements to cut themselves out a farm and brought out a wife and raised a family."

Sven thought of the train route that had brought them through the mountains from Baltimore harbor. He pictured young men the age of Isaiah Green or Bill Sutherland coming through the pass on horseback into woods as dense as the forest where loggers had not yet penetrated.

"Grandfather Anderson told me about going into the forest in Sweden to clear a farm with his father."

Mrs. Bates played the organ while her husband and the teamster sang hymns Sven had never heard. It seemed strange to see the teamster in a house, fresh as a man from town in his brother's spare clothes. Bates had often joined in the singing in the shanty on Pinch River, but here he seemed like a different man, his face smooth and calm. Sven wondered if before his wife died, the teamster had a home like this, if he had a Bible on his table and sang hymns with his family. Bates was different from many of the men in camp—more patient, more of a thinker. Sven wondered if Bates was a teamster instead of a lumberjack because he liked to come out of the timber and be part of this world.

When Mrs. Bates turned around on the swivel organ stool, her husband took up the Bible from the lamp table and began to read a story Sven remembered about a sick boy Christ had healed when his father begged for help. To his surprise, the storekeeper asked his brother to pray for them, and Bates did. When he finished, Mrs. Bates showed Sven up a narrow staircase to his narrow bed in a narrow room.

But that narrow room felt wonderfully spacious, as if there was room for all his dreams, for Mama and Lesja and Papa, for the younger children, and for a thousand singing angels. Never in Sweden had his family prayed. They never sang hymns, though Swedes were great for singing, and there were many churches in which many Swedes worshiped and sang. Mrs. Bates was a grandmother. Maybe if he had had a grandmother or if his parents had been able to read . . . He grew drowsy vaguely wishing for something he had never had. Something sweet like the smell of Mrs. Bates's kitchen and the herby smell of the pillowcase under his head. Something as real and physical as that throbbing in his chest with every heartbeat.

Once Sven awakened during the night. He could hear the melting snow dripping from the edge of the roof above the window near his head. Spring was well on its way. He went back to sleep to dream about a farmhouse where Mama sat with a large Bible in her lap. And strangely, Mama was reading, glancing up from time to time, smiling at him.

*   *   *   *   *

The trip back to camp was slowed by melting snow. The sleds' runners sometimes cut through to the road where the road was in full sun, and even in wooded places there was little shade, for the trees remaining were maple and aspen and birch, their branches bare. They had not reached Bates's shack by dusk, so with a nearly full moon bright on the snow, they drove on after letting the teams rest. The moon was straight overhead when they reached the shack. Soon after dawn they were again on their way. Even then, they did not reach the Pinch River logging camp before supper. Bill Sutherland and the bull cook came out when they heard the horses outside the cook shanty. Sven dropped down from his load and unhitched his team. His first duty was to feed and water the two teams.

"We saved you back some roast venison and apple pie," the bull cook called from the open shanty door.

When Sven returned from the barn, the supplies were already stowed indoors, and a plate filled with hot food was waiting on the small table next to the stove.

"The boss figures we'll have the timber down and get the loggers out by the middle of April," the bull cook told Bates while he poured his tea. "He expects to have the logs on the water by the first of May. But we can't depend on that."

Bates nodded while he chewed. "But with the last snow on top of what we had all winter, we'll have heavy runoff. Water in the Pinch should be high enough to carry our cut down the sluices into the Grand."

The bull cook pointed to the pie. Sven nodded. He reached for the pan and dished out two slices for himself and passed the pan to Bates.

"The Grand River is the puzzler," the bull cook said. "You know it, and I know it. We can have too much water moving too fast, and we can have quick drops in water depending on rains. You've seen it happen."

"It's those railroad bridges in Grand Rapids," Bill Sutherland put in.

Sven was listening, but he didn't understand half of what they said.

"Well," said the bull cook, "I'm headed for Chicago when we break camp. I have a fine wife who says no more log drives for me. I'm about ready to let her talk me out of logging camps entirely. I'm past the age for logging camps. Think I might try a little restaurant downtown. My wife's good at keeping books, and if I keep it small, I can manage the kitchen on my own."

Bill Sutherland laughed. " 'Small,' the man says."

Sven tried to imagine the bull cook stirring a small pot in a small kitchen.

When Sven entered the shanty, Papa was not with his usual crowd playing cards under the lantern next to the barrel stove. Harrington was leaning against the support post at the middle of the building. He nodded to Sven and then motioned toward the end of the shanty, where Papa's bunk was beneath Sven's.

Sven felt a pang of fear. Had Papa been hurt?

"I don't know what the trouble is," Harrington muttered when Sven stopped beside him. "He went straight to his bunk after supper. He didn't look sick. He's been working as hard as the rest of us all day."

Sven ignored an argument between Jamie and Arnie, ducked under the rope strung with drying socks, and went to Papa. He was resting with his back toward the wall, his pale eyes wide open and bright in the shadows.

"Has something gone wrong?" Sven whispered in Swedish.

"Nothing," Papa whispered in return.

"Do you feel sick? Did you hurt yourself in the woods?"

"Nothing is the matter," Papa repeated. His lips trembled, and at first Sven thought he had been drinking, but there was no whiskey on his breath. Papa grinned, and then his face went suddenly sober again. "Soon Pinch River Camp will close down. Then we'll be done with logging. Everything will be all right, Sven." He reached out and gripped Sven's hand and squeezed until the knuckles hurt.

The door at the far end of the shanty opened, and Bill Sutherland stuck his head in the door. "Nine o'clock!"

Sven stood on one foot to unlace one boot and then the other. Papa said no more, and Sven knew that unless Papa wanted to speak, asking questions would bring no answers. He threw his boot up to the foot of his bunk and climbed up. He shucked off his woolen trousers and settled under his blankets. Though he was tired to the bone, he could not go to sleep. Had Papa been thinking about the changes that had come over him in the camp? Had he decided to quit gambling and drinking? Had he lost so much money that he was now in despair and not himself? Had he received a letter from Sweden with bad news and decided to keep it to himself? Had something happened to Mama or Lesja or Karen or baby Peter?

Sven did not sleep, and neither did the bedbugs. He felt them traveling in a circle around the snug neckband on his long-handles seeking a fold through which they could tunnel and reach his body. There was no use pinching them. He had learned that long ago.

*　*　*　*　*

He was in the barn milking soon after four in the morning. There had been another down turn in the temperature. Though he and

Bates had broken through the slushy snow time after time the day before, the whole forest creaked, and even inside with the animals warming the air with their big bodies, his hands ached with the cold when he took off his mittens. Shivering, he washed the cows one by one and milked them. He had dreamed all night about the family in Sweden. If Papa had word and he did not, the news had not come from Lesja. Something must have happened to Lesja. Lesja, the strong one! Lesja, who in a year would be twelve years old. He gave each cow another forkful of hay and loaded his sled. His boots and the sled's runners crunched through the brittle ridges that had yesterday been slush thrown up by the big sled.

The greasy spicy smell of sausage floated to him before he passed through the golden lamplight streaming from the cookshack window.

"Ten below," the bull cook said when Sven set the shotgun cans filled with milk next to the heat while he prepared the strainer cloth over the ten-gallon can in which the milk would remain until the cream had risen.

Sven stood for a moment, watching as the bull cook pulled a giant baking sheet of golden brown biscuits from the oven and began sliding them two dozen at a time onto large heated stoneware plates.

Bill Sutherland chucked two sticks of wood into the cookstove's firebox and then straightened. "I had my heart set on spring and trilliums blooming along the river under the maples."

"You're drawing two dollars every day you're here," the bull cook said. "It's a sight easier work than what you'll get when the drive starts. There won't be any trilliums blooming along the Pinch River this year, and that's a promise."

"Why won't there be?" Sven asked.

Bill shrugged. "He's right. You'll see."

Sven washed his face and combed his hair. He noticed Bill Sutherland's grin. He remembered that the bull cook would soon be home in Chicago with his wife. He remembered Bates's sister-in-law in her neat house. He remembered Mama's whitewashed kitchen on the farm in Sweden when he was a little boy. Bill Sutherland took up the tin horn and headed out into the ten below zero outdoors. When he blew, Sven was already seated in his place at the table, nearly starved. He turned on his bench, watching the door for Papa. One hundred men and seven boys filed into the dining room and silently took their places. Papa came last and sat rigidly in his place. He did not look toward Sven.

The food was passed, and each man dished out his portion of biscuits and sausage and gravy, stewed prunes, and oatmeal porridge. Bill Sutherland made his rounds with the two-gallon coffee pot, and the loggers passed the cream pitcher. Sven buttered a biscuit and began eating his oatmeal. Papa still did not turn to look at him. The meal ended, and the men filed out. Sven circled the shanty, hoping to find Papa before the loggers left for the woods.

Harrington was harnessing his team when Sven reached the barn.

"If you're still worried about your dad," Harrington said, "I can tell you what's eating at his guts. He's been losing pretty regular playing cards, but lately he's learned some things, and day before yesterday he cleaned out some of the men who've taken his money all winter. Don't know just how much money was involved, but your dad came out with some big winnings and then refused to play last night. There was some who didn't take that kindly."

"Oh," Sven said.

He wondered if Papa owed a great deal at the company store, if he had gone straight there and paid off his bill. If that was so, then Papa might have no money now and could not deal into the card game. He wondered if Mr. Harrington had thought of that.

* * * * *

The cold held through the morning. When Sven leaned for a few minutes against the tar-papered door on the south end of the cook-shack, only the back of his neck felt the warmth of the black surface.

He went on the sled with flaggins to the woods at midday, and even then snow had melted only on the south side of the shanty and the cookshack, and the sled road was as solid ice as it had been in January.

"April! Can you believe it?" Bill Sutherland marveled.

The men came from the woods irritable and surly after dark. Already the season had lasted three weeks beyond what they had expected, and they were tired of cramped, filthy quarters in the shanty, body lice, and bedbugs.

"This place is worse than the barn," a young Norwegian from Iowa muttered as he waited in line to wash his face at one of the four washbasins just inside the shanty entrance. "Cows get clean bedding morning and night. My bed ain't been changed since Christmas, and the man under me sleeps in the same underwear he wore into camp in November. We stink like a styful of swine."

"You call us swine?"

"So we're swine?"

A Pole and a Mainer shouldered the Norwegian out of line and glowered at him.

"No offense," he said. "I just like clean living. I'm used to clean living. My mother won't know me when I get home."

"You're worried about your mama. Ha! She'll laugh and sing and make up your bed. It's the married man who has somewhat to worry about," said the Mainer. "I've had two wives put me out on my own when I come home flea-bit and crawling with lice. Your mama never forgets you're her son, but a wife can get used to making her own way with her husband gone all winter. A willful woman will."

After supper Papa was in his bunk again, his back pressed against the log wall, his eyes staring from the shadows. Sven sat on the edge of Papa's bunk and watched the men milling around the stove, hanging up wet mittens, a few washing woolen socks and wringing them out.

The card game began, and Papa shifted but did not sit up. Outside, the wind rose, and two men who had been passing a jug of whiskey began a loud argument. One took the last swig from the jug and threw it along the floor. Almost at once the other man slugged him in the chin, and they set into a wrestling match, tumbling closer and closer to the door. Finally, three loggers jumped up and, when Noodge McUftee opened the door, rolled the wrestlers out into the snow. They closed the door quickly and one logger reached to bar it.

"You can't do that!" yelled the Mainer. "It ain't human. It's cold out there."

"We're swine, the man said," shouted the Pole.

Jamie caught Sven's eye and grinned.

Few of the loggers paid attention to the brief shouting match.

Bates took a book from his safe box and leaned against the bunk nearest the fire under the lantern where light was good. Sven watched the pages of the teamster's book turn. Another loud argument began but fizzled into banter while two choppers whittled. Curls of birch fell from their pocket knives. One of them started a story but lost inspiration and fell silent.

The card game went on. The fiddler and a man with a harmonica started a dismal song about a man who went to war. He left his dog. He left his sweetheart. He left his mother. Stanza after stanza a yarder with no teeth kept singing, until the fiddler stopped for a drink from the water bucket.

Sven listened to the wind wailing along the eaves of the shanty and wondered about the men outside without their coats. The bull cook might have let them into the cookshack.

When the fiddler returned, he set his fiddle under his chin and started a jig. The harmonica player put his harmonica in his pocket and stepped out into the space next to the barrel stove and began to dance. But he hadn't the wind to keep up and dropped to a nail keg panting. The fiddler picked a faster tune.

Isaiah Green rolled off his bunk and stood up. He stepped into the open space and tapped the heels of his boots a few times; then he began to jig, his face as stiff as an ice-encrusted muffler.

The fiddler played faster, and Isaiah, with back as straight as a pike pole, his feet flying, looked straight ahead. The tune finished, but the fiddler did not pause. The next jig grabbed the heels of the last, and Isaiah kept dancing.

"Now ain't he a handsome man!" Arnie Bledsoe yelled from his bunk. He swung down and shambled down the middle of the shanty, pretending to jig.

Sven held his breath, for he saw Isaiah's eyes turn, though his body and head did not.

With a movement too swift to follow, Isaiah lunged for Arnie.

Sven took a deep breath and bit his lip.

The two boys rolled twice with legs flying. Arnie was on top for an instant. Then Isaiah was on top, pinning Arnie to the floor, crashing his shoulders and head to the floor time after time. Arnie bucked, and they rolled again, and when they turned, Isaiah's nose was dripping blood. Arnie broke free and smashed a fist into the bleeding nose, and Isaiah tripped him and landed on top of him, his knee in Arnie's chest. Arnie groaned. Sven knew the broken ribs had hardly healed. But Arnie had started the fight, and Isaiah was bound to finish it. When Arnie was too weak to fight back, Isaiah got up and walked out of the shanty.

Sven thought he should go to Arnie. But no one else moved, not one of the loggers, not one of the other shanty boys. The fiddler put his fiddle away, and one of the men threw a chunk of wood in the barrel stove. Finally, Arnie rolled over and rose on his elbows and his knees. Slowly he rose to his feet. He staggered to his bunk and pulled down his coat. He got his arms in the sleeves and headed for the door.

Sven unlaced his boots and pulled them off. Bill Sutherland stuck his head in at the door.

"It's nine o'clock in the swamp!" he yelled.

The lantern had been blown out for several minutes before Isaiah Green came back. Sven heard him set an armful of firewood beside the stove before he went to his bunk.

* * * * *

When Sven went into the barn with his lantern at four in the morning, he found Arnie burrowed in hay in the path between the horse stalls and the milk cows. Sven hung the lantern on its peg and began cleaning out the cow stalls and feeding them. When he came in with a forkful of hay, Arnie was sitting up.

One eye was blackened and swollen nearly shut.

"I'll just have me a little milk," he said. "I'm not going back down there."

Sven washed the two Jerseys, and while he milked one, Arnie squirted milk from the other into his mouth.

"I'll get you some food from the cookshack," Sven offered. "Do you want me to get your gear?"

"Obliged," Arnie said.

The cold weather had eased somewhat. Sven wondered if Arnie would walk back to Grand Rapids or to another logging camp. He'd need more than a handful of biscuits and a slab of fried salt pork.

* * * * *

"Arnie had it coming," Noodge McUftee said when the boys gathered to eat their noon flaggins apart from the loggers. "He always did talk too much. I figure hardly a man or boy in the world that don't talk too much, but Arnie in particular. I thought he'd learned after tangling with that Swede."

"Wonder where he's gone to," Jamie said, his face more sober than usual.

"Somewheres." Noodge grinned. "There's always somewheres else to be if one place don't work out."

Raf refilled his tin mug with coffee.

"I thought your mama disapproved of a growing boy drinking coffee," Jamie commented.

"Mama tells me I got to keep warm," Raf said. "Coffee's the hottest thing on the grub sled."

Sven finished his cornbread and bean soup. The soup had been hot. His belly felt warm and satisfied, though his hand was cold from holding the steel spoon. He helped Bill Sutherland stack the coffee mugs and the soup bowls in two washtubs. Then as the sled started back for camp, Sven picked up his ax and followed Jamie to the cuttings.

"For all his talk about his pa and brother, I don't guess Arnie's got folks," Jamie said. "He's in no shape to work, and no bosses is hiring now with everything closing down. It's too soon for him to hire onto a drive. Any boss looking him over can see he's not half himself."

"Yes," Sven agreed.

Jamie swung his ax at his side. "Myself, I got nobody in the world but in the camp. No family, no friends except here in Pinch River Camp. The hog boss has been good to me. Three years I've been with his crew. And Bates is a good man. I like him particular too. And the bull cook. Summer I do drives and hang around the mill towns earning a little. Now if I was beat up like Arnie is, that would be big trouble for me. But then, I know when to pick a fight and when to mind my own business. Arnie don't."

Chapter 8

From Landing Into Pinch River

The snow had sunken to a thin, compact sheath that melted each day and froze solid as ice each night. They had come to the end of the first week of April, and by rights the logging season should have ended. Everybody said so. And yet, if they loaded the sleds in the afternoon, they could still get them out on the haul roads before noon the next day. A few men had demanded their McEllroy pay slips and left. Nearly all the others were talking of leaving.

"It's too dangerous with the ground like walking on wet glass," a toothless Scot said Friday on the walk back to camp from the swamp. "I'm past my prime, but I'm not ready to die."

"I've got crops to get in back home," an Indiana farmer muttered.

Others echoed his statement.

Sven had been tallying his earnings in his head. Two dollars a week. One week in October. Nine counting November and December together. Thirteen counting January, February, and March. If he had two weeks in April, the company would owe him fifty dollars. Through supper he thought about asking Bates to put the money in the bank for him. His worn clothes would see him through the drive. He and Papa would work for a farmer through the summer and buy new clothes and put more money in the bank before logging started up in the fall. He was startled when the McEllroy superintendent marched through the cookshack and clapped his hands for attention.

"We'll clean out every standing pine on this tract or I'm no logging superintendent," the man told them. "We can't count on another week—three days at the most. What do we have left? Ten acres. Some of it maple along the lake. I want every man of you putting out one hundred percent. I'll give ten dollars extra to each man who holds out to the end."

Sven looked at Papa, who was sitting stiff and straight. Papa would stay. Of course, nobody replied. The no talking rule came from the bull cook, and even the superintendent didn't challenge that rule except to make announcements.

Saturday was a warm day from dawn until dark. Sven shortened his chores and went to the woods midmorning. He lit into swamping with the other boys, all rushed more now because Arnie was gone. Sunday they worked a half day—during the morning while the frost held the sled roads firm. During the afternoon men were too tired to boil laundry or sing. The loggers sat around the fire in the shanty talking about summer work. The boys went to the shop and sat around the fire talking about the season past. In October nine of them had come to camp early to help with the chores of setting up camp. Bobby and Sam had left to help out at home. Arnie was gone. Isaiah's nose was even more crooked since his fight with Arnie. Raf had gained around the middle and worried that he would grow stout like his father. Jamie needed new boots but was determined to wear this pair through the log drive.

"I'll be in the river all day. Why ruin new ones?"

"I'm going home to Allegan," Noodge McUftee said. "My dad wants me to make a fence around the cornfield. It's not just our cows getting into the corn. There are neighbors coming in with cattle."

Bill Sutherland was no longer one of the boys. The bull cook had already delegated real authority to him, and Bill wore his bowler hat indoors and out.

*   *   *   *   *

Monday morning the temperature was twenty degrees when Sven came back with the milk at five. He went to the woods immediately after breakfast. They had fresh beef and gravy for supper. Tuesday morning he found the red cow was gone. They had steaks with their biscuits for breakfast. Sven didn't even want the gravy. At noon he ate his stew and tried to chew the chunks of beef with potatoes and rutabagas. Thursday the black-and-white Friesian was gone.

Friday the air was warm and moist when Sven left the shanty in the dark. The sled pulled hard through softened packed snow coming downhill from the barn with just one shotgun can filled with milk. A misty rain began midmorning. The hog boss called off sledding. Instead, each teamster broke up his team, and one of the boys was assigned to each extra horse. They joined the skidders, taking the logs one at a time all the way to the landing.

The work was slow and frightening, with the huge draft horses struggling to keep their footing in the slush. Sven ran alongside one of Bates's horses as it lunged in its harness, the log gouged into the thawing earth and slush, then rolled. There were fewer than a hundred trees left standing, and the choppers and sawyers worked at a fevered pace. Noodge and Isaiah were swamping for all of them. Sven heard the shouts as he guided the horse on a shortcut between haul roads.

"TIMBER!"

Five trees down since he hitched up this time.

"TIMBER!"

One more coming down. Sven heard the crash and then a chorus of shouts that could only mean a man was under the fallen tree. Mechanically Sven continued to the landing, helped the yarder unhook, then set back up the haul road for the cuttings. He didn't allow himself to wonder which of the Jersey cows would make the next beef. He didn't want to know who had been injured or killed. He didn't want to see the body.

The saws were singing through wood again and choppers whacking at the trees when he reached the work area. The rain had increased.

Water dripped from the brim of his cap. It ran down his nose and dripped from his jaws.

"TIMBER!"

Another pine dropped.

"TIMBER!"

Another.

Sven backed his horse to the butt of a sixteen-foot log. With help from two buckers, he secured the chain and took up the reins.

Water pooled in the hoofprints in the trail. He made two more trips before Bill Sutherland came with flaggins. He joined the others around the sled and took a bowl of stew and a slab of cornbread dripping molasses. After the food was passed out, Bates helped Bill move the kettles and tubs to one side; then Harrington and another logger brought up a body wrapped in a sheet of canvas.

Sven saw an elbow and a shoulder too small for a grown man.

"Who?" he asked Bates.

"Noodge McUftee," Bates said. "I'm sorry, Sven."

Sven turned his back and ran splashing from the sled.

"TIMBER!"

He stopped instantly to see where the tree was falling. He watched it crash across the unpiled limbs and tops of trees already cut into logs and yarded to the lakeside.

Noodge McUftee killed. Noodge was going home to build a fence to keep cattle out of the cornfield. Not now. Was he going home to Allegan wrapped in canvas with his pay slip pinned to the package?

Before dark the last tree was down, the last log yarded. Some of the men ate supper before they left camp. Others simply picked up their slips promising pay when the timber was sold. They tramped down the slushy road in a light rain, shouting to the men ahead of them and laughing with others walking with them.

"You better buy yourself some new britches," Harrington advised when he passed Sven outside the office shack. "You look like your mama sewed you into that pair in the fall before you started growing on the good grub."

Sven said nothing about buying new pants. His feet hurt in his boots, but he had made up his mind not to buy anything against his wages. That money must be saved. If he earned cash for work in town, he'd buy an outfit. He followed the two teamsters to the toolshed at the end of the horse barn. Finally, he began milking the two remaining cows. He strained the milk into a single shotgun can and put on the lid, then watched Bates secure the tailgate in Harrington's wagon.

"It's raining now, but the road still has enough frost in it to hold up my team," Harrington said as he and Bates loaded Harrington's wagon with equipment he had brought into camp in October. "I've bought the smaller Jersey," he told Sven. "Lead her out since you've finished milking. I'll just tie her to the tailgate here."

Sven felt a rush of joy. "I'm glad!" he said.

Harrington smiled. "She's too fine a cow to butcher. My wife will treat her like a queen."

Sven stared at the one remaining Jersey. "Won't the men on the drive need milk? Couldn't we just take her along on the riverbank? I could picket her twice a day and keep Bill Sutherland happy with butter and cream."

Bates grinned. "It's up to the bull cook. The cows were charged to kitchen expenses. Harrington talked him into keeping both Jerseys alive through the last day in the woods. You try your talking on him. He's been on enough drives. He knows how much depends on men getting fed right."

And so the last Jersey was spared, and though some of the crew talked about fresh beef the following days, they liked their cream too.

By Monday the camp was empty except for the men who would take down the buildings. For the whole week the camp resounded with nails screeching as men using crowbars tore up plank floors and roofs, first from the cookshack, then from the shanty. Papa and Sven joined six men and Jamie to sleep on scrap hay spread thickly on the floor of the feed room in the barn. Bill Sutherland had gone but would be back in two weeks when the drive began.

For now the workers fared however they could, cooking a big pot of beans every second day over an outdoor fire, drinking milk by the quart, and frying flapjacks in the biggest skillet over coals.

The hog boss himself was gone, and Bates was in charge of preparations for the drive as well as the teardown. Sven cleaned out the horse barn, and all the tools were brought down from the shop to be stored there. The hog boss had taken the company books and the last few shirts and socks from the store. Shelves were nothing but planks, which were now piled with the other lumber that would be moved up river to next season's camp when the roads were dry in June.

The fiddler was gone. The gamblers were gone. Papa seemed less fearful, but he said very little, and Sven worried even more than before that Papa had received bad news from Sweden and was keeping it secret.

And then the last day of April, Bates slipped Sven a letter with his own name written in Lesja's careful script.

"A timber agent brought up some mail this morning," Bates said.

Sven did not ask Bates if he could take off to read the letter. He grabbed it and ran down a muddy skid road and sat down on a maple bowed under a pine top. He opened the thin paper carefully, for the letter had been folded to make its own envelope. The Swedish words were cramped tightly.

Dear Brother Sven,

The winter is bitter in Stockholm. We have not had money for fuel. Mama has been sick. Grandfather is very ill and says he will not live. I am afraid he knows the truth as old people often do about such things. We cannot stay here after he dies, for he had the rooms only as part of his pension as a soldier. Mama does not know what we shall do. Karen has gone to live with Mama's cousin in the country, for he has only sons and has always wanted a little girl. We shall not see Karen again. She is to take the cousin's name and will be

Karen no more. Mama says this is best, for the cousin has a fine farm and plenty of good food and a warm house, though his wife is not a generous person. What will become of Peter? No one will adopt a little boy with crooked legs.

I have had no more letters from you. Are you well? Is Papa well? Mama says with you both working so hard and far from the city, we cannot expect letters. But I long to hear from you, Sven. Each day I pray and so does Mama. We can do nothing else.

Your sister, Lesja

Sven read the letter time after time. He folded it and carefully placed it in his shirt pocket. When Papa came from demolishing the office building, Sven stopped him.

"There is a letter from home," he said in Swedish.

Papa's face turned pale, though he was sunburned.

"What does your mama say?"

"Lesja writes that Grandfather will die soon, and then they will be out of a place to stay. They are all sick."

"Read it to me," Papa said. "Read it all."

While the others washed and started drinking coffee beside the fire, Sven and Papa stood on the west side of the barn where the sunlight was still strong enough for reading. Papa listened. "Read it again," he said when Sven finished.

"So Karen has gone to Cousin Oscar Kostarson?" He brushed his sleeve across his eyes. "When did Lesja write the letter?"

Sven found the date finally, cramped into the margin where glue had torn away all but the month. "January."

"A great deal can happen in four months. By now the old man is doubtless dead and buried, and what has become of your mother and Lesja and Peter? If you write to them, where do you send the letter?"

"Lesja can still write to us," Sven said. "Bates will bring mail to us on the log drive. We may get another letter soon."

Papa was silent for some time.

Sven had been thinking for days about a clean bed with sheets, a washtub with hot water for bathing, and clean clothing. "Can we go back to work for Mr. Schmidt when the drive is done?"

"It's two hundred miles," Papa said. "I might work in a mill in Grand Rapids. You could work at something there too. We could rent a room."

"I liked the Schmidts," Sven said.

Papa did not reply.

*   *   *   *   *

Papa had built a twenty-by-twelve-foot raft with a twelve-by-twelve shack on one end—a wanigan, the men called it. Bates set Sven to work cleaning this new wanigan, which would go down the river behind the drive. On it Bill Sutherland would cook meals for the drivers, and on it many of them would sleep. It was finished now and sat on blocks beside the river. Sven swept it, scoured its shelves and floor, and scrubbed the rust from the lids of its small cookstove. Bates brought three lengths of new stovepipe and an elbow. Sven fitted the pieces together, one length attached to the stove with screws and extended through a tin-framed hole in the wall, the elbow just outside, and two lengths turned up and held steady by wire loops. When the ice on the river turned to slush along the banks, Bates and Papa knocked out the blocks and eased the wanigan down to its skids.

Agents had been through camp along with scalers. All the logs waiting for the drive had been scaled and marked. Now there was nothing holding up the drive except ice in the river. Water had been running in a swift, black stream down the middle of the channel for more than a week, but along the banks, ice rose and fell with the current. Then the water rose more than two feet above the ice, and within hours the entire stream was open, with great chunks of ice grinding against each other. They built up at the curves in the river then broke loose and rushed on their way.

The McEllroy superintendent was in camp the morning the first team of drivers set out along Pinch River. Sven watched as he directed the men with peavey poles loosening the first pile of logs on the skidway. The pile shuddered when the first log rolled down, and then a driver loosened the key log at the front of the pile and jumped back quickly. The pile began to roll almost magically, and then with a rumble, it cut free, and the logs flowed into the water, the current pulling them away as drivers kept the pile sliding, rolling.

"We want plenty of open water so they don't jam up," Bates said. He watched with Sven for a few minutes, then turned back to lowering the wanigan, one block at a time, to the level of its own log skidway.

"You been down the river before?" the superintendent asked Sven, who was hitching Bates's team to the haul chains attached to the wanigan, which rested now on the skidway twenty feet from the river's edge.

"No, sir, I have not," Sven said. He straightened and tried to look as manly as possible, though he realized his clothes showed right off he'd had a big growing spell since he bought them.

"You'll use the muscle you've put on this winter," the superintendent said.

Sven was glad the man had not asked his age. Drivers were supposed to be sixteen. He'd had a birthday in the late winter, but he was now just past thirteen. He wasn't as tall as Papa's six-foot-one frame, but he figured with the food he'd get during the drive and on a farm during the summer, he'd pass Papa. Grandfather Oldstrom, before he began stooping, had been a giant of a man, and Mama was tall.

The log drive was a venture in which all the logging companies on the Grand River and its tributaries took part. Each company got its timber into the water and headed downstream. The superintendent was here to see that McEllroy's Pinch River timber, which accounted for more than half of all the logs on the Grand drive, got a good send-off.

Chapter 9

From Drive to Pileup

Bates's team was hitched to the haul chains on the wanigan when the teamster came with Bill Sutherland and a redheaded Norwegian named Thorsten.

"Sven, you hold the horses' lines but leave the orders to me. These girls have done this job before and understand."

Sven had heard Bates say half a hundred times that those mares had more sense than half the loggers in camp. Now he held the leather straps loosely in his right hand and moved as far to the right as he could while the Norwegian sloshed water on the peeled skidway logs. Thorsten stepped back.

"Get up there, girls. Up and easy," Bates said in a low voice.

The bay mares stepped forward and leaned into the harness with a shift of their weight that tightened the chains. The wanigan creaked. Thorsten dashed another bucketful of water onto the logs.

"Easy," Bates repeated, and the horses stepped ahead and leaned their chests into their collars. The wanigan began to move just as a sled loaded with logs would move on the icy sled road.

"You have that rope hitched?" Bates asked Bill Sutherland.

"With ten feet of slack," Bill Sutherland said.

The horses reached the water and walked in at Bates's command.

"Let out another ten feet of rope, Bill," Bates said.

When the wanigan finally floated, it swung slowly in the current. Bates unhooked the pull chain, and Sven brought the team around. They stood dripping and shivering. Sven took them to the barn and rubbed them dry. Only then did he begin to understand how cold he himself would be during the weeks ahead, in the water time after time each day.

By the time Sven got back to the wanigan, Bates had secured the houseboat to a second tree on the bank and brought down a twenty-inch-wide plank and set it like a bridge.

"Come along, Sven," he called. "Let's load it with supplies for the first part of the drive. Flour, dry beans, cornmeal, lard, salt pork, prunes."

Sven laughed. He had already made his own inventory, and he had seen Bill Sutherland's check sheet. To Sven's surprise, Bill appeared with a wheelbarrow that had a wide, flat bed and a narrow iron-rimmed wheel. Instead of two men packing the heavy tubs and boxes between them, Bill loaded them, and Sven trotted down the plank, pushing the load through the door.

"We'll feed off this wheelbarrow the way we handed out flaggins off the sled in the woods," Bill explained.

When they had hauled on the last of the supplies and pots and tin plates and mugs, Bill lifted the wheelbarrow and hung it on pegs driven into the outside wall of the wanigan.

"I asked Bates if he'd let you be cookee on this drive," Bill said. He grinned, and Sven grinned back.

He guessed there would be chances soon enough to become a river pig, but after walking the horses out of the river today, he was willing to put off that part of the work until the ice was out of the lakes upstream and the water warmed up. There was the one Jersey cow to feed and milk. And once the grass sprouted through the matted brown along the river, he would have to picket her. Sven could see he'd be busy enough that even a visit from the McEllroy superintendent would not alarm him.

He discovered that his work as cookee began immediately, for Bill

Sutherland hollered for kindling and then firewood. Smoke was pouring from the new stovepipe when Sven trundled the wheelbarrow with a second load of maple and birch stove wood. He stacked the wood on the plank floor beside the door to the floating cookshack.

He also discovered that a daily chore would be "looking beans," spreading dry white beans on the table and picking out any dry hulls, small lumps of dry soil, and tiny rocks before rinsing the beans and delivering them to Bill to be soaked overnight. The next day Bill would keep the large pot of beans boiling at the side of the cookstove from daybreak until supper.

"Be cheerful," Bill said. "I've been a cookee since I was your age, and now I get to be bull cook. In five years you could know enough to keep a logging camp running in top condition. Never forget, Sven, a logging operation runs on its grub. And beans is a cook's best standby. I know a hundred ways to fix beans."

Sven laughed, but cautiously. Bill Sutherland had been one of the shanty boys only two weeks earlier. But his position had changed. Now he was a man to be respected, even by seasoned loggers and drivers.

*　*　*　*　*

The first day of the drive, Pinch River filled with logs, all carried wide of the wanigan by the current. From the small window over the worktable inside, Sven saw loggers on their feet riding logs, running across the moving mass, jabbing here then there with their poles to loosen up a pileup. Once he saw Papa.

The men trudged back to camp to eat in the wanigan and sleep in the horse barn again. Sven's bunk was above Bill Sutherland's, next to the cookstove.

The second day of the drive, Sven laid the cookstove fire before milking the cow. He hurried back with the milk and strained it at the cookshack door. The foreman was inside.

"We got the logs past the first slough yesterday," the drive foreman told Bill Sutherland.

Bill, who was stirring oatmeal porridge with one hand and nudging sausage about in a skillet with the other, did not turn around. "How many days you guess we'll hold on here before moving down to the next hitch?"

"Maybe a week. Maybe more."

"How soon will you have me eggs?"

"Not until the next hitch," the bull driver said. "With muddy roads. You know how it is."

Sven skimmed the thick cream from the second shotgun can on the deck outside. Twelve drivers arrived, quickly ate their oatmeal with cream, their sausage and biscuits, and then they disappeared upstream. A half hour later, logs began to stream by. At noon Sven helped Bill Sutherland wheel beef and boiled potatoes with gravy and pie to a makeshift plank table on the riverbank. The food remained out for nearly two hours while three or four drivers at a time jumped to shore and filled their bellies before moving on downstream. At dark another hot meal was ready, often beans fixed according to one of Bill Sutherland's recipes, usually including brown sugar, molasses, and salt pork.

The first ten days of the drive were rather like that first day. Then on the eleventh day, the bull driver ordered the wanigan downriver to the next hitch. All the logs from Pinch River Camp were now ahead of them. Sven hauled extra stove wood and finally led the Jersey cow on board the raft and tied her next to the wanigan shack with a generous supply of hay.

Until they were midstream, Sven had not realized how shallow Pinch River was. Though the water was still icy cold and he had no desire to get in, he guessed he could wade across almost anywhere.

Thorsten manned the rudder at the rear of the wanigan. A man stood at each forward corner with a pole to push the raft off from any sandbar or submerged log and to guide the wanigan around the oxbows where the river nearly doubled back on itself while flowing through nearly flat, swampy land. The river bottom itself looked as if it had been scoured clean. Even the willow brush along the marshy banks looked combed. Sven rolled piecrusts at the table under the window and watched their progress through maple groves all bright red with blossoms, through birch thickets and matted willows pressing to the water's edge, and through reed beds flattened by the run of logs. Smoke from the stovepipe streamed past the window, and an occasional spark floated in. Sven slapped a round of piecrust into each of a dozen pans, dipped a pint of stewed dried fruit from the kettle on the stove, and carefully laid another round of crust on top before crimping the edge. He'd watched Mama do it. And Mrs. Schmidt. Finally he slashed two steam vents in the top crust and handed the pies into the oven. Sven was forever licking his fingers and tasting. Bill Sutherland noticed, but he only grinned.

Sven stoked the cookstove fire time after time, for as soon as the pies were out, the beef roast went in. It must be done when the wanigan came to shore at its new moorings at Cedar Point.

"Get that cow off at once," Bill Sutherland ordered when the raft had been tied up and the plank bridge laid on the sandy spit of land.

When Sven untied her, the cow bolted, and though he held to the rope, she jumped into the water. Sven ran three steps on the plank before she pulled him in behind her, and together they splashed onto the damp sand. Sven tied her, brought the remnants of her hay, and went back to clean up the mess she had left on deck, first with a shovel, then with hot water, lye soap, and a brush. After the noon meal, he found the horse shed, the pen, and the haystack.

That night when the last of the drivers straggled back up the river, Sven was excited to see Jamie among the men.

"I've been on McEllroy's Allen Branch drive," he said, swaggering a bit as he took a tin plate and filled it with beans and took a slab of cornbread. "We brought the timber down three sets of rapids in ten miles without a jam-up. Slick as pouring gravy over the lip of a pan. I rode the logs all the way and didn't get wet. Not even my boots."

Sven wanted to tell his friend that he'd made the pie, but after Jamie's account of taking the rapids, he kept still.

"You been on the water yet?" Jamie asked when he saw Sven scurry to help Bill Sutherland.

"I've got to be cookee for the first half," Sven said, cutting another pie and setting it on the plank table.

"Good pie," Jamie acknowledged with his mouth full. "We've been eating pretty shifty grub on the Allen drive. Mostly what the men could cook in one big iron pot banked with coals all day. Doubt it ever got washed. Just poured in more water and started the fire all over again with gritty beans and a few chunks of salt pork." Jamie took up the crimped edge of the crust in his fingers. "Good pie."

*   *   *   *   *

Cedar Point was upstream on Pinch River less than half a mile from the mouth of Allen Branch. While Jamie claimed the logs had all come down Allen Branch, Sven could see logs backed up in the slough beyond the point. He didn't have to ask how the lumbermen would get back across the branch as they walked back to the wanigan for supper and bed. When he looked, their boots were as dry as Jamie's.

"There's a herd of deer in the cedar thickets around the slough," Jamie said the next noon when he came in to eat. "They've yarded under the old growth with the trees so tight together and the branches so thick overhead they might as well be in a barn. They browsed off all the green tips as high as they can reach standing on their hind legs. You ought to see it, Sven. If I had a gun, I could bring in some venison."

"Not for me to cook," Bill Sutherland said. "The bucks are tough and rank any time of year, and the does are all carrying fawns unless they've already dropped them. And the fawns wouldn't make any more meat than a snowshoe rabbit."

"There's yearlings," Jamie said when Bill walked away.

"There's fish in the backwaters, and I've heard that redhorse are running in the streams too small to float logs," Bill said. "I'll give Sven a chance to put some fish on the table in a day or two. I brought along a spear."

Jamie shrugged, but Sven saw he was envious.

* * * * *

During a brief break between washing gravy grease off tin plates after breakfast and peeling shriveled potatoes for the noon meal the next day, Sven asked about the fish spear.

Bill got it from under the worktable. "Better practice hitting a dead leaf on the sand," he advised.

After sufficient practice to satisfy Bill, Sven stuffed an empty horse-feed sack inside his jacket and tied a slender rope to the spear and to his left wrist. Then he set off running across floating logs for the first time. As long as he ran fast enough, he felt no more anxious than if he had been running on packed earth. When he came to open water, he stopped abruptly, and the log under his right foot rolled over. He sat down suddenly, and one leg went into the water before he flipped over and got back on both feet. He planned his path to the isolated raft of logs floating in a small inlet, moved swiftly from log to log, and then jumped four feet across open water to the raft, caught his balance, and kept moving. He jumped finally to land and found a dry path through tussocks of dead marsh grass along the four-foot-wide channel where crystal water flowed over a gravel bed.

He had no idea what a redhorse looked like, but he saw fish moving upstream, their silver sides reflecting purple and green and gold when they passed from sunlight to shade and back into sunlight. He took careful aim. His first try brought a two-foot fish that he thought might be a lake trout. He put it in his bag and set the bag several feet from the water. Though he aimed as carefully time after time, it was a half hour before his next success. Then, in a few minutes, he had as many fish as he could carry. The stream was suddenly filled with silver backs, fins slicing the surface as they jostled each other for space to move out of the river toward some small pond.

With the spear, Sven nudged a log close enough to shore to swing his sack ahead, jump, teeter for a moment on the slow-turning log, then balance along it to the floating mass.

Going back to camp was slow business, for instead of running, Sven had to heft the load of fish from one log to the next. He found that if he settled his feet down in a certain way, logs did not spin. That was reassuring.

"You build the fire," Bill Sutherland said, obviously pleased with Sven's catch. "I'll clean the fish."

When he saw how carefully Bill did his work, Sven understood why he had been sent to make a fire on the sandy beach.

Long before dark, the fire had burned to a huge bed of coals, and Bill showed Sven how to "plank" an entire fish, nailing its opened body flat to a wide slab of freshly split cedar, then standing the slab near the fire to broil the fish.

"I could smell that trout cooking a mile down the river," the Norwegian Thorsten said as he washed his bare arms to the elbows in the tub of warm water set on a barrel near the supper table.

Sven had already eaten all he wanted before the men returned from the drive.

After the fish were finished off, along with biscuits and stewed potatoes and bean soup, Papa sat down on a block of wood near the glowing bed of coals. Sven went to stand beside him. He knew Papa was remembering the hundreds of meals for which Mama had cooked fish at home in Sweden: salmon from the streams when they lived on the farm, and codfish or herring when they lived in the city and bought it in the market. They had hoped for another letter from Lesja, but none had come. Had Grandfather Oldstrom died? Were Mama and Lesja still together? How was little Peter doing? Had Karen already begun to forget she was an Anderson with a mother and a father, brothers, and a sister?

For the first time Papa and six other men bunked in the wanigan. Jamie Laughton and the others walked downstream to a shack used by the Allen Branch drivers for the past two weeks. Sven watched Papa talking to the bull boss on the raft outside. The lantern light fell across Papa's shoulders, but his face was in the dark. Their voices flowed along smoothly with no rise or fall. The bull boss came in and washed his face with hot water and took off his boots. Sven scrambled up to his bunk over Bill Sutherland's and watched for Papa. The others were in bed when Papa came inside and closed the door. He turned the lamp down and stood watching the flame die and the narrow band of red-glowing wick darken. Then he too took off his boots and dropped into his bunk.

More than anything, Sven wanted to talk with Papa, to ask him how much money they had saved up and where they would keep it safely through the summer and through the next logging season. He wanted Papa's arm around his shoulders so he wouldn't miss Mama and Lesja so much. But it seemed that Papa purposely avoided the times and places where they might talk, times they could just be together.

Sven realized that Papa had tried all winter to match the roughness of the loggers in the camp, to hold his own among men used to lots of whiskey and lots of fighting, gambling, and other things they quit talking about when he walked into the shanty. Sven guessed Papa had to do that to earn the respect of the toughest men in the camp. But Harrington never sat around drinking whiskey, and he didn't gamble. Sven couldn't remember seeing him with a pipe either. Nor Bates. Neither of these men had been worried about the opinion of the loggers, and yet everyone seemed to respect them. And both of them had been as anxious to look after him as if he had been one of their family. But Papa . . .

Sven rolled over in his bunk and faced the raw pine boards of the wanigan's wall. He wouldn't let himself think like that. He took breath after breath of the resinous air, still warm from the cookstove fire. In the slough the frogs began to croak, and finally the whole night vibrated with their singing.

* * * * *

Here at Cedar Point, Sven again milked before breakfast, cleaned up after the loggers had finished, and looked beans for an hour before he began paring potatoes. A few days after their arrival at the Point, Bates came up river with a bateau loaded with fresh supplies, including eggs. Now the flapjacks were light because Bill Sutherland added eggs to the batter. There were fried eggs and bacon, cornbread, and custard pies.

"You pay attention, Sven," Bill said at least once each day. "You'll be a regular cookee in camp next year. I'll tell the superintendent myself I believe you can handle it. I'll buy you a black hat myself."

Sven laughed. Bill never wore his bowler hat on the wanigan, and likely in the fall he would take to wearing a white cloth hat while cooking in the new camp. Sven was tempted by the prospects, for a cookee spent winter days inside the shack. He got first chance at all the best food, and he earned top pay. And yet, much as the idea appealed to him, Sven took a peavey down to the water each afternoon and practiced walking the logs, prying grounded logs from sandbars, jumping across gaps, and running to keep his balance. He hoped that soon he would get to join Jamie and the drivers on the water.

Pinch River was covered bank to bank with logs, and the slough below Cedar Point was covered. Allen Branch logs were all down, the drivers said, but the drive was being held back because companies on other streams flowing into the Grand were ahead of them, and the big river was full all the way to Grand Rapids.

"We'll be in a fix if the water level drops with us spread out like this in the slough," Thorsten said as he greased his boots beside the fire one evening.

From what he said, Sven pictured the Pinch logs riding like a shifting raft held together by the margins of the slough, with two or three drivers working a few hundred at a time into the moving water and riding them down five miles to the next holding place. Behind them came two more drivers with a few hundred more logs. At the end of the day, all the men tramped back upstream for their hot meal and a few hours of sleep.

When the wanigan moved on down the twisting, turning stream, the bull boss gave orders to tie up well ahead of the last part of the drive. Here there was a shack for the men and a fenced lot with hay for the several teams of draft horses and the cow.

"There's rough water ahead," Jamie told Sven at suppertime. "The boss is afraid of a jam-up. There was a big one at the rapids last year, and then the water went down. There wasn't much left we could do until June brought heavy rains. He don't want any more of that."

In late May, daylight hours were long, and in the drive camp, men, who had worked since dawn and left the river only when darkness fell, ate and went to bed almost at once, too tired to joke or yarn or play their harmonicas.

"What's that wriggling in the water barrel?" Sven asked Bill when he dipped water to heat for washing the tin bowls and plates one morning.

"Mosquito wigglers," Bill said.

"What's that?"

"You'll know soon enough," Bill said.

Wigglers were in the shallow water where Sven brought the cow for her drink that evening. Two days later when he hunched just before dark beside the Jersey to milk, her tail swished steadily, and he heard a faint humming sound. Then on his ears and the back of his neck and then on the backs of his hands, he felt a hundred stings. He stopped milking and swatted, then waved his arms to drive away the cloud of insects. When he strained the milk, the cloth held the dark spidery shapes of hundreds of drowned mosquitoes. Bill tacked filmy white cloth over the windows of the wanigan, and the door was shut. The drivers huddled close to the bonfire, even standing in the drifting smoke to avoid the swarms of mosquitoes, while they hastily ate their supper. The next afternoon a driver helped Sven start a brush fire upwind from the horse pen. On this fire they heaped damp young swamp grass.

"That smudge will save the beasts a lot of torture. They'll just line up in the trail of smoke and stand there all night."

And then a driver named Mosier twisted an ankle. He insisted the sprain wouldn't keep him off his feet but a few days, and he was a man the hog boss didn't want to let go.

"Sven Anderson," the hog boss said that day, "give Mosier your paring knife. He can sit on a stool and help out here. It's time you got started out on the river."

The boss sent him to work with Thorsten a mile down Pinch River where the roots of a newly fallen elm fanned out into the water. Logs were standing upright in the water with others crisscrossing among the roots. Thorsten showed him how to loosen a key log so that those behind it could float free.

"You stay right here the rest of the day," Thorsten told him. "Any timber comes by, keep it moving. When you get a break, pull out a few more jammed logs. Whatever you do, don't lose the peavey."

Pushing off the moving logs was fun. Working on the pileup was work, and more than once Sven found himself waist deep in the water. He was thankful that although it was cold, the ice had been gone for nearly a month now. Since he was in and wet, he pulled and heaved on a log tangled in the twisted roots until he freed it, and it bounced through the tangle and floated away. Grasping the peavey, which he had stabbed deep into the sandy riverbed, he jumped to the tree trunk and from that position jimmied log after log free before the next sizable raft of logs floated around the bend toward him. Sven was now a river pig.

The sun was down and the air was thick with mosquitoes when the last logs bobbed by, and by then the trapped logs were cleared out. Sven was certain he had had it easy on his first day driving. He was right about that. Before the end of the week, he was with the main crew, scrambling from one mess to another, from one bank of the river to the other. On Sunday, the logs started down the rapids. Sven went with them, riding out the first quarter mile of tumbling water on a three-foot pine that broke through everything it plowed into. Where the current slowed, another driver yelled and waved him over, and he dashed across bobbing, rolling logs to help the other man free a sixteen-footer that had lodged in the bank with rapidly moving logs piling up behind it.

In minutes the jam blocked Pinch River from bank to bank. A half hour later Jamie Laughton arrived with a team of dappled grays, and Sven helped a driver secure a chain to the end of the troublesome log.

The bank was low and muddy, and the horses had trouble getting solid footing, but they struggled with all their weight into their collars, jerking the log one direction and then another until it came out of the bank with a sucking sound. Sven unhooked the chain and joined nine drivers scrambling over the jammed logs, looking for one here, one there that when released would set others behind it free. They were working with late afternoon sun glaring on the water until they could hardly see when their logs came around the final bend into the holding slough.

With Jamie, Sven trudged back up the river, glad that where it came through the rapids it was almost straight and that here there was a trail. He ate his pork and beans and cornbread and molasses and still had room for pie, but he was too tired to enjoy the food. Mosier had taken over his bunk on the wanigan. So he tramped with Jamie back to the shack, where a smudge poured a wide stream of smoke through the open windows. Though his blanket was too warm, he pulled it over his head with only a breathing hole, and even then a few mosquitoes found their way in. In the morning his nose was swollen with more bites than he could count.

*   *   *   *   *

As everyone had feared, the river began dropping rapidly, for the lakes and swamps upstream had drained off the last of the snowmelt. Pinch River ran less than fifty feet wide, and even there the channel was shallow. Drivers carefully maneuvered a clutch of logs at a time around the bends toward the rapids, where rock ledges now lay bare with a few narrow spouts pouring from one pool to the next. Sven stood with his peavey on such a ledge, back far enough to be safe from tumbling logs but near enough to step forward with outstretched pole to nudge a stranded log back into the water before others piled up.

The entire winter cut was past the rapids before the first of June, and the bull driver was full of praise for the crew.

"There's nothing but good to report to McEllroy. Nobody hurt to notice. The horses all in fine shape. We'll have all our timber into the mill's holding ponds in two weeks." The wanigan came down. They had fresh beef for supper and beef stew the next day, but no cream on their oatmeal porridge. Sven guessed the Jersey cow was gone.

That day a draft horse slipped on a muddy bank and went down with wild screams. Its right back leg was broken. The bull driver shot the animal, and the men pulled the huge body out of the way, using the other horse of the team to do the job.

"Losing a good horse is as bad as losing a man," Thorsten said when he saw Sven standing there.

"Why did he shoot him?" Sven whispered in horror.

"A broken leg don't ever heal," Thorsten said. "Not in an animal that heavy. Only decent thing to do is to put an end to its suffering fast."

*   *   *   *   *

The water was sluggish now where Pinch River flowed into the Grand. In two days it had dropped enough that thousands of logs lay in the mud in marshy areas. Where they could, the river pigs waded in a few inches of water, floating log after log free.

Finally, the bull driver gave the men a few days off to go into Grand Rapids.

"Clean up. Have a good time. But it if rains hard for more than a day, I want every man of you back here on the job."

Sven watched the drivers take their pay slips from the bull driver and set off over the floating logs toward town.

"You stay here," Papa told Sven in Swedish. "You can make yourself useful tending to the horses. Bring your bag into the wanigan. The cook won't leave."

Papa explained that he would use this time to look for summer work in the lumber mills. "I'll be back to help finish the drive," Papa promised. "McEllroy pays drivers better than mill hands."

*   *   *   *   *

"Some of the men won't come back," Bill Sutherland told Sven while they ate fried fish and boiled potatoes alone that evening. "The boss knows it, but there's nothing else he can do. He don't want twenty idle men spoiling in camp. They'll go into town, lay down their pay slips for half their value in the saloons and hotels. They'll get drunk and roar and fight there, spend all their money, then drift on somewhere else to work for a bed and grub until the camps sign on in the fall. Me, I'm saving most of my earnings with McEllroy in the bank. The bull cook saved most of his pay every year. He's got ten thousand dollars saved up now for his eating place in Chicago. He's forty and can do whatever he wants. I'm saving."

*   *   *   *   *

Jamie disappeared with the other drivers, but he was back on the wanigan in three days. He'd been with teamster Bates's brother, who owned the shoe store.

"There's a letter for you," Jamie said. "I wasn't planning to come back yet, but I knew you'd want to know what was in the letter right away."

Sven took the envelope, remembering that Jamie had no family at all.

The message was from Lesja. Peter had gone to a home for orphans. Mama was washing and mending for a merchant's family. Lesja herself had found a place as an upstairs maid in a great house. She had a small chamber over the kitchen that was never warm, but once she left her room for the family's quarters, she was comfortable. The housekeeper had a short temper. The butler was stiff and disagreeable, but the children whose rooms she kept were cheerful, and their mother treated her kindly.

"I worry about Mama," Lesja wrote. "She has been so long with poor food and worries all the time about Karen and Peter, and tall as she is, she looks so thin. She works so hard."

Lesja mentioned no hope of coming to America. There was an address. Sven determined to write to his sister the following day, though it might be weeks before he could get the letter out to the mail.

"Why don't we both go back out to the Bates's place?" Jamie suggested. "Mrs. Bates can find chores for us to do—cutting grass, cleaning up around the sheds, spading her vegetable garden. You could mail your letter."

Papa had said he should stay, but Sven told Bill Sutherland his plan and set off with Jamie.

Mrs. Bates stopped them in the yard and had them strip down in the wash house. In clean clothes, they came in for a good meal.

"Stay as long as you like," Mrs. Bates told them.

Sven basked in her cheery grandmotherly affection, something entirely new to him since both of his own grandmothers had died before his birth. With Jamie, he sat with her two or three times each day listening to stories affirming God's care for her and her family, her faith in salvation, and her admonitions to give their lives to serving God.

"My grandmum was a Christian," Jamie told Sven their second night sharing the upstairs bedchamber. He looked a bit awkward when he spoke, but when he asked Sven if he wanted to pray before they got into bed, Sven nodded. Jamie did the praying, but Sven took note of how it was done.

Before breakfast, Sven had written his letter to Lesja.

Mrs. Bates went to the post office with Sven's letter while he cleaned horse stalls and spread rotten manure from the pile behind the barn on the side of Mrs. Bates's garden, which had not yet been turned. Instead of spading it, Sven and Jamie hitched up one of the horses to a small turning plow and plowed and then harrowed the garden. They helped her plant green beans and squash and corn, all crops Sven remembered from the Schmidt garden in Indiana.

When it began to rain, Mrs. Bates rejoiced for her newly planted seeds. When it poured down the second day, she began to worry that the rows might be washed away entirely. With rain still pouring down the third day, Sven and Jamie set out for the wanigan, perhaps five miles from town if they walked upstream on the floating logs. The logs were treacherously wet, and water poured down Sven's legs into his boots. He was certain that everything in his bag was wet too.

The bull driver and four other men had already joined Bill Suther-land at the wanigan when Jamie and Sven arrived. They peeled down to their skin on the deck outside, shivering as they rinsed under the water pouring off the wanigan's roof. They stepped under the shed roof overhanging the door, and Bill handed them each a pair of his own dry pants.

"The river's up more than a foot," Jamie informed the men sitting on the bench in front of the cookstove, drying their feet.

The bull driver clapped his hands with satisfaction. "We'll be ready to move timber by morning. By then, rain coming down fifty miles from here will be pouring down the Pinch. Let's hope a few more drivers show up, but if they don't, we'll drive without them."

Sven noticed that Mosier was stretched out on the bunk that had been Papa's. Mosier must have made a full recovery if he was one of the first drivers back.

"Sven, climb over these longshanks and help me rustle some sup-per," Bill Sutherland said. "There's hot water. Make them all some tea. Then we'll set to flipping flapjacks. Good thing we still have molasses."

Though it was mid-June, the air was chilly, and the men agreed that even if it was crowded, everyone would sleep in the wanigan. At first light they had finished their breakfast, and with peaveys in hand, they stepped off the wanigan onto the river of logs. Although the logs had risen with the climbing water, they were still not moving downstream.

"I don't like this," the bull driver commented when they came to the mouth of the Pinch and surveyed the stalled logs blocking the Grand around its next bend. "With this much lift, everything should be moving as fast as we can walk."

By sunrise they could see the problem. Logs from another company had come down the Grand River unattended during the night and had lodged in the first railroad bridge.

Of course, hundreds of townspeople and mill workers stood along the banks shouting in great excitement. A locomotive with a train of lumber puffed black smoke at the bridge approach for a half hour. Twice the engineer blew its whistle, then finally backed off.

"For certain, the railroad's worried about this," Mosier commented. "We won't break this one up with dynamite. Not with the bridge at stake."

"The question is, can the bridge withstand this much pressure?" the bull driver said.

Though the logs causing the trouble belonged to another company, every company now had logs in the jam. Soon every experienced driver on the river was on the logs, each man jabbing with his peavey, some with coils of rope thrown over their shoulders.

"This is no way to manage things," the bull driver said to a man in a top hat and a white shirt, who had come across the logs to inspect the situation himself.

"You're right about that," the man said, tipping his hat to another man dressed in business attire. "Spencer," he called, "who's the best man you know to put in charge before half of these reckless fellows kill themselves and take out the bridge in the bargain?"

"Thomas Mosier's the man," Spencer said without hesitation. "Wish I knew where he was."

"He's working for me," the bull driver said. "He's here somewhere—wearing a red flannel shirt and green galluses."

CHAPTER 10

From Disaster to Home

Fifty men wearing red flannel shirts and drab green galluses were climbing the mountain of logs. Sven spotted Mosier on the railroad bridge stepping along on the crossties, stopping every few paces to peer down at the jumbled timber below. The bull boss saw him, too, and waved to him, but Mosier did not look back.

"That's your man," the bull boss told Spencer and the man in the top hat.

Spencer waved down a driver passing by. "That's Thomas Mosier up on the bridge. Go tell him he's wanted."

The driver took off up the street.

Sven watched the conversation when the messenger reached Mosier. Mosier continued walking toward the far side of the bridge, and the messenger came back.

"Your man says he'll take a look at the far side. He'll be back directly."

"McEllroy, I would advise you to get all the men off the pack," Spencer told the man in the top hat.

Sven was startled. The man looked important, but not important enough to be owner of the logging company.

Mr. McEllroy walked away with Spencer, and the bull boss called Sven and Jamie to follow him up off the timber to the street. Before the noon whistle blew at the sawmill, drivers were lined up in crews, each with a leader, and all the leaders were standing ready to take orders from Mosier.

"I think they ought to blow up the bridge," Jamie said on the third day. "It's shook loose in the pilings anyway."

Mosier had other ideas. Sven heard about the master driver's plans wherever clusters of people gathered to watch the drama on the river.

According to Mosier, a few key logs were holding back the front of the logjam. Expert drivers worked on freeing any logs at the front that they could separate. Meanwhile, several crews upriver were put to work chaining off sections of the mass of floating logs into booms to keep them from following when the jam began to move. Nearer the bridge, other men would wrestle the piled-up logs into some kind of order, trying to remove the gravest danger to the bridge pilings.

Sven watched from the north end of the bridge while men with saws and axes attacked the crisscrossed timber below. Spencer and McEllroy were always there, calling down to Mosier from time to time and listening carefully to his replies. Mosier himself worked in the most dangerous position, with carefully picked men helping him. Log after log was cut in half, the sawed-off pieces thrown into the river to float away. Logs that had been held back by that one log's upthrust end were eased loose and moved off.

For three days the two boys tramped down the floating logs to watch from the street. Each evening in the long twilight they walked back to the wanigan for grub and a bed. On the fourth day, Mosier sent everyone but his small crew off the river; then with half the townspeople watching in horror on the banks, Spencer himself threw down two long ropes from the middle of the bridge. Mosier's helpers tied the ropes to his body, shook his hand, then backed off a good distance. Men on the bridge, standing seventy-five feet apart, tied the ends of the rope to the railing, then gripped the rope where it still hung slack and pulled it tight. They let out a little rope at a time as Mosier eased himself down the jumbled logs. He raised his ax to chop through the upright log that he believed would release the entire pileup once it snapped off.

The excited shouting hushed. Sven, like all the other people in the crowd, was listening so intently for any sound of breaking timber that he hardly dared to breathe. The ax rang as it threw broad chips from the pine log. Mosier shifted to chop from the opposite side. He stepped back slightly and studied the face of the logjam. With his pike pole he wrestled a single log so that it leaned heavily against the top of the log he was chopping.

"Are you ready?" he called to the men above holding the ropes.

"Ready! Ready!" two voices called back.

Sven saw Mosier lean forward, testing his balance, and then the driver raised his ax and delivered a mighty blow.

Sven heard the log break and saw its severed end fly into the air as the log behind it crashed down. Mosier took up his pike pole and maneuvered another log free, then jammed down hard on the top of the log he had just chopped in two.

Suddenly there was a creaking sound and then a roar as the front of the logjam exploded between the central pilings of the bridge. The bridge trembled, and one of the pilings gave way. The bridge with its crossties and tracks began to sag. On either end the crowds moved back to make way for the few workmen who had remained to watch from the railings and now scrambled for safety.

A cheer rose from the crowd, but the sound died suddenly, for no one yet knew what had become of Mosier. Sven thought certainly Mosier had been smashed and was even now floating downstream among the bounding giant logs.

And then a single voice shouted, "There he is! There's Thomas Mosier!"

Mosier was climbing one of the ropes.

He limped a little as he walked off the damaged bridge between the two men who had jerked him from the logjam just as it had started to move.

"Sorry about the ax and the pike pole," he told McEllroy, who reached out to shake his hand.

"I was afraid we would lose more than a peavey," McEllroy said.

The crews above the bridge had been ready. Now every driver in town was on the river. Sven ran with Jamie upstream a quarter mile, where they grabbed peaveys from the tool wagon. Then they jumped across open water to the moving mass, pushing, shoving, and straightening logs not headed with the current.

Ahead of the boys, more experienced drivers struggled with leaping logs set free when logs beneath them slid away in the current. This was deadly business, but all the men rushed into it as if this were a party, laughing and shouting to each other, their red flannel shirts flashing as they leapt and ran.

On the water in earlier days, Sven had been surprised that the huge logs floated without rolling. He and Jamie had practiced birling just for fun, purposely rolling the log underfoot and practicing keeping their balance. Now Sven was quite certain he would be content to ride a stable log, but many of the logs he landed on had been knocked wrong-side up and rocked and rolled over and just kept on rolling as they floated toward the bridge.

Jamie was beyond him now, working his way to a pile of logs floating like a raft, swinging in the current and headed for the damaged bridge support. Sven waited for a large log to come by, jumped to it, and then to another. He reached the pileup before Jamie and began working to topple the first log off. It swung dangerously then rolled down the pile and floated away.

"Good work!" Jamie shouted as he jumped on board.

Together they broke down the raft to a single layer of logs with two lying crosswise. "I don't want to be riding this thing when it hits," Jamie said. "It could just be enough to bring down some ties and tracks on our heads."

Sven looked to see if another free-floating log was near enough for them to jump to. "Let's just get one more log loose and ride it," he said.

Together they heaved with their peaveys. The log teetered, almost balanced. "I'll get it," Sven said. He thrust his peavey under the shorter end and heaved. The log swung violently, stopped, then swung back. It caught Sven just above the left knee. He heard the bone snap as he fell backward into the water, still holding his peavey.

The pain broke over him as if it were the water itself. When his head bobbed above the surface, the water dragged on his legs, and the pain doubled. Sven concentrated on his grip, for the twelve-foot pole was buoyant, even with its iron point.

"Hold on!" Jamie yelled.

Sven looked up just as the great log swung again. Jamie jumped out of the way and broke its balance, sending it into the water on the far side of the raft.

"My leg is broken," Sven said.

"Can't be," Jamie said. "Hold on."

He pried a single log free, pushed it toward Sven, and then leapt to it himself.

The water sucked at Sven's heavy boots and the loose legs of his pants.

"Get on the log," Jamie told him.

Sven let go of the peavey pole with his left hand, and the water pulled him under. He stretched to reach and caught hold again.

"I can't," Sven said, gasping.

Jamie flipped, landing on his back in the water and kicked hard with both feet. The log rolled once and settled inches from Sven's shoulder. Desperately Sven thrust his left arm over the log.

"There," said Jamie, swimming toward him on the opposite side of the log. "Just pull yourself up. We'll ride her under the bridge and then make for shore. You've still got your peavey."

Sven directed the pole toward Jamie's hand, and Jamie took it from him. Then with both arms over the log, Sven tried again and again.

"I can't do it," he said, hardly above a whisper. "I can feel the bone wobbling in the water."

"You have to," Jamie said. "I'll come around and—"

At that moment, the remaining logs in the raft struck the bridge. Sven looked up to see a section of track with crossties attached swing down like a ladder overhead. Helpless, he clung to the log as it floated slowly beneath the collapsing bridge toward the bank to their right.

"I hit bottom," Jamie said hoarsely. "Water's not more than six feet deep here. Hold on, Sven. Don't let go of the log just because your feet touch."

"The boy's hurt," someone shouted on the shore. Several men scrambled down through brush into the mud, wading out to meet them.

The log was less than twenty feet from the water's edge when Sven's right boot struck the bottom. He braced himself with that leg, but the log swung, and he fell backward, the log floating over his head.

The men pulled him ashore.

* * * * *

Sven came to lying on a table with brass pots suspended from a white board near the ceiling. The ceiling itself was white. Three men in tall white hats stood on his left, and on the opposite side stood the bull driver.

"Well, Sven Anderson, so you've broken your leg," he said.

The pain engulfed Sven's whole body, but he could feel that his left leg was bare.

"We cut off your pants," the bull driver said. "I hate to do this to you, son, but there's no help for it. I have to set the bone. The cooks here gave me two smooth paddles they use to take pies out of the oven and enough clean cotton towels to bind you up right."

Sven thought of the draft horse with its leg broken three weeks earlier. He remembered its wild screams of pain and terror. "The horse," he whispered.

"Don't plan to shoot you," the bull driver said. "Jamie's gone to see if he can find your father. Heard he works at Spencer's mill. It's not far. But we might as well go ahead. I've set as many broken legs as anybody in this town, doctor or no."

Sven clenched his fists at his sides and bit his lips, determined not to scream no matter how bad it hurt.

The men in white hats moved in, one on either side and one to his right foot. The bull driver nodded to them, and they got hold of his arms and ankle. The bull driver grasped his left leg just above the knee and leaned back.

Almost like the water flowing over his head in the river and the river's current dragging on the broken leg, Sven felt himself going under. But he could not open his mouth. He would drown if he opened his mouth. The water was pressing him down to the river's dark bottom. The water was dragging him along the muddy bottom, and over his head twenty-foot pine logs passed one after another, and finally everything grew dark.

"Thank God we had some ether," one of the cooks said.

Sven felt his body rotating. Perhaps it was the table rotating with the men in tall hats walking around in a circle as the table turned slowly.

Papa was standing beside him and reached now to take his hand.

"It was a bad break," Papa said in Swedish. "The bull driver says it will heal, but slowly. Maybe in six months."

"But I have to work," Sven said. "What about Mama and Lesja and the little ones?"

Papa shook his head. "We have our own troubles now. We are in trouble almost as great as theirs."

CHAPTER 11

From Papa to Battle Creek and Beyond

Papa had a room in a boardinghouse that he shared with three other men who also worked in Spencer's mill. Jamie and a man Sven had never seen before helped Papa carry him on a stretcher made of two peaveys and an old tablecloth donated by the hotel cooks on whose worktable the bull driver had set Sven's leg.

Though they were careful, and Sven could see that they were, he was in an agony going up the boardinghouse stairs. The shabby third-floor room was smotheringly hot, though the tiny window was open. Four narrow cots filled nearly the entire floor. Four pegs in the wall held jackets and pants.

"I got to get back on the drive," Jamie said when Sven was settled on Papa's cot. "I'll come by and see how you fare tomorrow."

Sven nodded. "Please bring me my sack."

"You cannot stay here, Sven," Papa said after Jamie had gone. "There is not space. It is not healthy. The landlady will not allow it."

"You could ask Mrs. Bates," Sven said. He knew the teamster's sister-in-law would take him in.

But when the other boarders returned that evening, Papa went down to his supper and came back with news. Blackburn, who shared the room, lived on a farm less than ten miles away. His wife and children were looking after things there while he worked in the mill, hoping to make enough extra money to put up a proper barn in the fall. Sven could stay with them, keeping an eye on the small ones while the woman worked outdoors.

Sven realized that this was a chance to be useful so that Papa would not have to put out much money for his keep. Yet going to strangers was fearful. He thought of his little sister Karen and pitiful little Peter. Indeed, he and Papa did now have their own troubles. Through the night Papa slept on the floor between two of the cots, for Sven was in his cot. Sven did not know whether the pain in his leg or the pain of approaching separation kept him awake.

"I have to get off to the mill," Papa said soon after dawn. He brought Sven a jar of water and handed him two small white rolls and a slab of cheese.

Blackburn stood beside Papa, buttoning his galluses to his pants. "I saw a neighbor's boy on the street yesterday late. He's driving out about noon, soon as he's loaded up his lumber for a chicken coop. He'll make a place for you on the load."

"Listen for the mill whistle," Papa said. "I'll get here as fast as I can after it blows at noon. I'll help the boy get you down to his wagon."

Sven lay in the bunk in too much pain to finish even the first dry bun, but he drank the water and wished he had more. He felt feverish. His clothes had not completely dried since he fell into the river. They smelled salty and rancid. As the room grew warm, he drowsed several times, waking up when a slight movement sent slivers of pain through his leg. He was lying there staring at the water-stained ceiling when he heard boots on the stairs. It couldn't be noon. The mill whistle had not sounded.

"Got my load stacked sooner than I expected," a young man said from the doorway. "If it's all the same to you, I'll just carry you on down now and get on the road."

Sven wanted to tell the redheaded young man he couldn't go until Papa came, but the boy just bent down and thrust one arm under his shoulders and one under his knees. The splint swung out straight and struck the door frame when the young man turned. Sven gritted his teeth and held his breath as the young man turned sideways in the stairs and worked his way down with his back against one wall.

With no more care than if he were loading on a heavy bundle of goods from the store, the redhead laid Sven upon the lumber, without so much as a rolled-up shirt under his head. The young man sprang to the wagon seat and spoke to the horses, who began to trot down the street. One arm on either side of his body, his hands pressing down on the warm lumber, Sven tried to hold steady, for each time his body rolled ever so slightly, the intense pain increased.

"I'm thirteen years old," he told himself. "Too old to cry for Mama."

But the whole ten miles to Blackburn's farm, Sven pictured Mama leaning over him, felt Mama's hands wiping the streaming sweat from his face and neck. There had been no chance to talk with Papa about the future. No chance to say goodbye.

Jamie had prayed that night after Mrs. Bates had talked to them about God's love and about getting ready for heaven. "God, are You still there?" Sven felt foolish, as if he were a whimpering puppy. Mrs. Bates had made God seem so near. If only Papa had sent him to Mrs. Bates. But what could he do to earn his keep there? He drew his lips tight over his teeth and breathed in long, steady breaths.

Mrs. Blackburn was hoeing her garden when the wagon came to a stop in front of her cabin. The redhead handed her a piece of paper. She took it and read it, then stuffed it into her apron pocket.

"I suppose if Mr. Blackburn says so, it has to be," she said. "Bring him in."

Sven tried to block everything out. The redhead took him up and carried him into the cabin. Mrs. Blackburn indicated the bench beside the fireplace. She stood there looking at Sven until he felt sick.

"I'm Sven Anderson," he said. "I didn't mean to break my leg."

"Of that I am certain," Mrs. Blackburn muttered. "So you're to lie still for the rest of the summer?"

The bull driver had said six months. Sven just nodded and tried to half sit up. "I could do something to be useful," he said. "I've been in the lumber camp since last fall until the drive. I've been helping the cookee and tending to the cow."

Sven noticed a small child asleep on the bed in the corner of the room. A cradle stood near the bed, and he guessed there might be an infant sleeping there.

"When they wake up, I could watch the little ones," he said.

"That you could," the woman said. "You could watch them do whatever they set out to do, but you couldn't chase after them and keep them out of the fire or from drowning in a tub of wash water."

"I could sit on a stool and rub clothes on a washboard. I could wring out the wash, everything but hang it out to dry."

The woman sighed. "Next week or the week after. I got work to do. Holler if the boy wakes up. His name is Socrates. The baby's Elisabeth, but she don't know it. If she wakes up, it won't matter to let her cry."

Socrates awoke soon after his mother left. He scooted to the edge of the bed, flopped over on his belly, and dropped feetfirst to the floor. Sven guessed he was two years old. Cautiously, Sven let himself down to the floor and waited for the child to come to him. Careful to keep him away from the splinted leg, Sven played with him as he had often played with Karen when she was a toddler and with little Peter. The baby stirred but slept on.

As the sun dropped toward the west, Mrs. Blackburn came with a pail of water and an armful of greens. She took the milk pail but said nothing to Socrates or to Sven.

"Bring me the greens," Sven told the little boy when his mother had gone to the shed to milk. "Bring me your mama's dishpan."

Though he scattered a few leaves along the floor, the child obeyed. Sven looked over the greens carefully, removing a few green cabbage loopers and flipping them into the coals in the fireplace. He wanted to wash the greens and put them in a pot to cook, but when he tried to pull himself up, he knew he could not.

* * * * *

After three weeks, Sven sat most of each day in a chair beside the table with everything he needed for his chores within reach. The remainder of the day he spent on the floor playing with Socrates or holding Elisabeth. They had no news from Mr. Blackburn, and though Sven had expected Papa would walk out to see him on Sunday, he hadn't come. Mrs. Blackburn was less sullen, but Sven could see it was her nature to be sullen about her lot in life. He knew he was making himself useful, doing more work for her than he made for her. July passed. Hot August began, and Mrs. Blackburn began to talk of harvesting the small oat field.

Sven offered to sharpen her scythe. Now he often sat on a low stool in the dooryard playing with the children while he shelled beans or peeled apples and sliced them. He watched Mrs. Blackburn mow the oats then twist a few bands of oat straw to hold a bundle together. After nine bundles, she shocked them carefully like small thatched huts. At the end of August Mrs. Blackburn began cutting the even smaller patch of wheat. She grumbled a great deal, for she was working very hard, but Sven knew she was pleased that the apples he had prepared for drying nearly filled a cloth flour sack hanging from the rafter above her bed.

"If you weren't here, my husband would be here cutting the grain himself," she said.

Sven said nothing. It did no good trying to be friendly with Mrs. Blackburn. Each night he slept fitfully on a tattered quilt on the floor. At mealtimes he was grateful for boiled young potatoes and an egg or a slab of bread. He drank his milk, grateful that Mrs. Blackburn had that cow.

In September the weather turned bitter for a little over a week, and then warm weather returned. Maples along the field turned red and gold, and then the leaves began to fall. Papa had not come. He had sent no message. Then at the end of the first week of October, Mr. Blackburn returned home.

"Is Papa coming soon?" Sven asked anxiously.

"Your father quit work at the mill the week after you got hurt," Blackburn said. "He gave me five dollars for your keep. I haven't heard a word from him since June. But you'll have to figure out someplace else to stay for the winter. I've taken off a week to thresh the grain; then I'm going back until the mill shuts down for the winter."

Sven listened in disbelief. He looked at the bare log walls and the gaping fireplace. He understood why Mrs. Blackburn said almost nothing, even to her children. This was their farm, but there was no joy here, no good fellowship, no love between husband and wife. But he knew that when Mr. Blackburn came home when the mill closed, Sven Anderson had to be gone.

But where could he go? Where had Papa gone? At that moment he understood that Papa had abandoned him. He knew now how Mama and Lesja must feel in Stockholm.

There was a horse, Sven discovered. All summer it had been hired to a neighbor. Now Mr. Blackburn brought it home and began hauling the oats and wheat from the field on a wide sledge. The oats he stacked like hay under a makeshift shed. Sven discovered Blackburn intended to feed the bundles like hay to the cow and a young steer during the winter. A threshing machine would pass through the community soon and would thresh the wheat for a share of the grain. The wheat and some corn from an acre, the ears hanging upside down on the stalks, Blackburn would carry a sack at a time to the nearby gristmill to be ground to flour and meal.

"I don't know why that woman hasn't kept you busy shucking and shelling corn," Blackburn said the second night he was home.

Sven saw Mrs. Blackburn look over her shoulder when her husband said that. She looked very tired and a bit fearful. Socrates looked fearful too. Elisabeth did not cry.

Mrs. Blackburn had brought him two forked maple saplings in September. Sven had cut off the double tops, stripped the bark, and smoothed the widely branched ends. He had contrived a sling into which he could slip his left foot when he stood up. The weight of the leg hung then from the forked crutch, and with the two crutches Sven could move about a bit. Most important, he could stand to do his chores and could work much faster than when he was sitting. Though his leg ached in the chill early mornings, he seldom felt more than a twinge once he was up and about.

Blackburn left at the end of the week.

"You've been kind to me," Sven told Mrs. Blackburn. "I want to be as much help to you as I can. Do you want me to leave now, or should I stay until almost time for the mill to close?"

"It's the food," she said, embarrassed. "You earn your keep and more, and you're company for me and the children. But Mr. Blackburn . . ."

"Then I'll find a way to town as soon as I can," Sven said. He did not want to bring Mr. Blackburn's anger down upon his wife.

The following morning he got up before daybreak. With a burnt twig he wrote a goodbye thanks to Mrs. Blackburn on the hearthstone and swung through the door and across the dooryard on his crutches. He stooped under the farthest apple tree to pick up as many small bruised apples as would fit in his pockets. By noon he had reached the public road, and a half mile beyond, a farmer in a wagon stopped and helped him up to the wagon seat. The farmer took him directly to the Bates's door and waited while Sven knocked.

"Just to be certain there's somebody home," the man said.

"Sven!" Mrs. Bates cried. She threw her arms around him and knocked his crutches flying.

He explained everything that had happened since the accident, although he tried not to blame Papa for leaving. "He's taken the troubles with Mama and the little ones hard. When I broke my leg, it was just more than he could bear."

Mrs. Bates wiped her eyes and cleared her throat.

"And you need a place to winter?" she asked.

He nodded.

She said nothing about bathing in the shed or stripping off his filthy clothing. She brought him straight to her kitchen table, set him down, and bustled to bring him bread and butter and a glassful of milk.

Sven smelled chicken roasting, and a small pot boiled on the range.

"Mr. Bates will be home at six," she said. "You shall have real food then, but now you must be starved."

Sven set the last withered apple on the table and grinned.

"Maybe I can find some kind of work in town for the winter," he said. "The bull driver said I wasn't to walk on this leg until January, for until it's really knit, it might break again."

"The Lord will provide for you," Mrs. Bates reassured him. "You will find a home with us, Sven, if you need us."

If only Papa had let him come here in the beginning instead of going to the Blackburns' place! And yet, there was some pleasure in knowing that Mrs. Blackburn had truly needed him, that he had brought some sunshine to the two small children whose lives were so dismal. He told Mrs. Bates only the better part of his experiences across the county.

"Bless you!" was all she said.

* * * * *

Mr. Bates's brother, the Pinch River teamster, stopped by a few days later, already hauling supplies to the new McEllroy camp ten miles beyond the previous year's location. The two Bates men had been talking about Sven's predicament, he could tell.

"Bill Sutherland is some put out that you bowed out on him. He counted on you being cookee for him," the teamster said.

"When you see him, please ask Bill if he's still got my bag," Sven said.

"Jamie Laughton's gone over to the Wisconsin woods," the teamster said. "Things isn't exciting enough for him here, he says."

Sven learned that Sam Duell and his half brother, Bobby Cooper, were already at the new camp clearing haul roads.

"Now there's the place for you!" the teamster interrupted himself. "Sam's dad's been laid up ever since he called for the boys to come home last winter. Pretty much taken to his bed, and Mrs. Duell's saddled with all the work around the place. If they didn't need the money so bad to pay off the mortgage, Sam and Bobby would stay home and help their ma. You're a good hand at milking. That woman's got twenty cows all pouring out the milk."

*　*　*　*　*

Bobby took off from work the following week and personally carried Sven in the teamster's wagon to the Duell farm near Battle Creek.

"Maybe I can't do much else," Sven told Mrs. Duell, "but I can milk cows. And I can sleep in the barn when there's snow and ice."

Like her sons, Mrs. Duell was a quiet person, infinitely patient and kindhearted. She brought out Sam's winter clothes from the previous year and opened the left pant leg and fixed it with buttons and loops so Sven could be properly dressed for the first time since his accident. She patched Sam's old coat and darned two pairs of worn socks. She handed him her husband's shoes.

"He don't know it, but he won't ever get out of that bed," she said sorrowfully. "I've been a widow before, and I can bear whatever comes, but Warren's such a good man. It will be hard to let him go."

It was his heart, she said.

"This once you stay in the house," Bobby told his mother after supper. "I'll show Sven how we do things. When I'm gone, you'll have plenty of time to do barn chores."

Sven hobbled behind Bobby to the large brick barn with its high roof. Mrs. Duell would feed the animals and carry the milk. Sven would just move with his milk stool from one animal to the next to milk. The milk cooled in tall cans in the spring house on the uphill side of the barn. Every day except Saturday a wagoner came by and picked up the milk, returning the cans in which the previous milk had gone to the large hospital in town.

"Sunday they pick up double," Bobby said. "Dad's a Saturday keeper like the Advents at the hospital." Sven did not understand what that meant.

But during the days ahead he got the picture. Mr. Duell was not a Jew, but he kept Saturday for Sunday. There were a lot of people in Battle Creek who shared his religion. Some of them came out to the farm to help with the work.

"Christians ought to help each other out," one gray-haired gentleman said as he stacked the firewood he had split on the porch.

Mr. Duell had a long shelf of books, and though he was no longer able to sit up to read, he told Sven he ought to be reading them. "Evenings are long, even if you've milked a barnful of cows," he said. "A man's mind gets hungry."

"Thank you," Sven told him, thinking of Isaiah Green and of Mr. Duell's own sons with their dreams of an education and a future that went beyond grinding labor and poverty.

Most of Mr. Duell's books were about religion or history. Among them Sven recognized the book Mrs. Schmidt had bought from the traveling book salesman—the book with pictures of beasts with wings and horns. He spent many evenings reading that book, stumbling over many of the English words, but forging on anyway. He was surprised that one chapter told about the history of the Christian faith in his homeland.

Snow fell in late November, but Mrs. Duell swept the path to the barn clear and walked beside Sven, fearful that he might fall. Friends from Mr. Duell's church came almost daily with cooked food. Women helped Mrs. Duell care for her husband, and men cleaned the barn, fed the livestock, and carried the milk.

"It's only a matter of days now," Mrs. Duell told Sven in a whisper one night. "Warren thought it best to sell the farm, for it is mortgaged to half its value. If I auction the cattle, there will be enough to send the boys to school next winter, maybe for several winters. Warren's set they have an education. There's a buyer for the farm. Warren signed the papers today."

And Sven saw that he would again be without a home. When the gray-haired man came to split wood the following day, Sven told him.

"Hold on," the old man said. "God will provide. Do not fear. Before you call, He will answer. While we are now speaking, He has prepared a path for you."

The old man's words were comforting, but the new owner would be arriving as soon as Mr. Duell was decently buried. Mrs. Duell would move into rooms in Battle Creek and work in the hospital. She had said so. The work would be easier for her. She would have conveniences impossible on the farm. And she would be with friends who would comfort her in her grief.

Warren Duell died the following Wednesday. Sam and Bobby came home and stayed to see him buried on Thursday. Sven helped them stow their belongings in wooden crates that would be stored in a neighbor's attic.

"It was expected," Sam told Sven. "We were ready. We had said our goodbyes. He can sleep in peace now. That's what matters. It's been hard on Dad, watching Mama work so hard. He's been right about the farm too. No matter how hard we tried, we could never get out of debt, and this way Mama has a start in town, and we get to go to school. Dad wanted me to become a doctor, you know, but I think Bobby will make a better one. I aim to go into business."

"I wish you boys could just accept the Sabbath truth," Mrs. Duell said several times. She wept very little except at the thought that they were returning to the Pinch River Camp, where they would work on Saturdays.

Bobby looked at Sven and pursed his lips. Sven figured there were more serious moral risks in the camp than working on Saturdays and was glad his friends' mother did not know about the violence, the gambling, the drinking, and the profane language. And yet, he could not bring himself to think that Bobby and Sam would be led into those temptations.

*   *   *   *   *

Sven had written to the Schmidts in Indiana, but, of course, he had not heard from them so soon. He went with Mrs. Duell to town and helped her unpack in the half of a house she had rented. He sent a letter for the teamster Bates with Bobby. If letters came from Sweden, Bates must be able to send them on.

In Battle Creek nearly everyone Sven met belonged to the Adventist church and kept Saturday with strict care. This meant woodboxes were filled early Friday afternoon, food was cooked before the "Sabbath" began at sunset on Friday, no games or frolic at all during Sabbath hours. But for the most part, while they were a sober lot, the Adventists were a kindly people. He might get used to being among them with time, even if they ate no meat and frowned upon the pies and cakes he had enjoyed so much on Pinch River. No coffee. No tea. Sparing of butter. A little honey, but careful of the sugar!

But Sven had managed at the Blackburn farm where even wholesome food was doled out with painful stinginess. There was nothing stingy about Mrs. Duell or her Adventist friends. He went with Mrs. Duell to meetings at the church and listened while she read the Bible each evening and prayed. At home in Sweden there had been no such concern for religion, though there were churches enough and people thought of themselves as Christians. He wondered, *If Papa had been brought up with the Bible and prayer and always knowing God was nearby and watching, would he have fallen so easily among evil companions?*

Sven began praying himself, first for Mama and Lesja and the little ones in Sweden, and even for Papa. And then for himself, that

God would make a place for him, provide him a home and work and a future.

* * * * *

December passed without Christmas fanfare. Mrs. Duell wore black. Sam and Bobby had taken off time for the funeral so did not come home again for the holiday. Finally, in early January when Sven was beginning to walk without a crutch, a letter came from Mrs. Schmidt. Yes, he could come. Yes, there was plenty of work, but he must go to school as well. She made that very clear.

With the few dollars he had earned since moving into town, Sven purchased a rail ticket. Mrs. Duell pressed his freshly washed clothes and admired him once he was dressed and ready for the trip.

"You've been a blessing to me, Sven Anderson," she said as she walked with him to the station. "A blessing sent by God to help me in my need."

"You've been good to me," Sven said. "A blessing," he added.

* * * * *

It had been well over a year since Sven and Papa had come into South Bend, Indiana, on the train from Baltimore. Now he could understand English and speak it quite well. He could even read in English, words that were familiar to him. He had grown nearly a foot, and even Warren Duell's old shoes were tight on his feet.

The first ride to the Schmidt farm had been dusty and hot. This trip was bitterly cold with a freezing fog hanging thick over the flat farmland. The team clattered over the frozen ground, and the wagon jolted over repeatedly frozen muddy ruts. Talk was difficult, and Mr. Schmidt was still a quiet man, but they were friends with a great deal of news to share.

One of the Schmidt daughters had married. One had moved to South Bend to attend college, for she planned to be a teacher. Otto and his two sisters were in school today, Mr. Schmidt said. Sven would go with them tomorrow. Everything was arranged. There would be no sleeping in the granary. He would share a room with Otto.

"You have heard nothing from your father?" Mr. Schmidt asked. "That seems strange. He must have had an accident himself. Will he be able to trace you here?"

"Bates knows," Sven said. "And Mama and Lesja in Sweden will know when they get my letter."

He did not want to tell Mr. Schmidt that Papa had abandoned him when he was helpless. He wanted the Schmidts to hold their good opinion of Papa. That seemed very important.

In the farmhouse kitchen, Sven pulled off his patched coat and let Mrs. Schmidt hug him. He ate a bowl of hot gruel, although he knew that in less than two hours the whole family would be sitting down to a heavy table.

"I've learned to cook," he told Mrs. Schmidt.

She shook her head. "Not in my kitchen, you won't," she sputtered. "With two daughters to help me, I should say not!"

Sven stood with his back to the kitchen range and let the heat soak into his body. The ache in his leg melted away as if it were made of ice. He turned and held his hands over the stove top, flexing his fingers. "I've been milking twenty cows morning and evening," he said.

Mrs. Schmidt began paring potatoes, rinsing and dropping them one by one into a pot on the stove. "That's better news. My husband has kept seven of his best heifers. They'll start milking in the spring. They will need more hay and more oats. Otto frets that it is unfair that his sisters share the housework while he has all the barn and field chores to do alone. You and your father spoiled him when you were here, you know. He has become lazy."

Sven laughed and Mrs. Schmidt laughed, too, at the very idea of anyone in this household being lazy. She rested one hand on the edge of the table and looked at him in a way that made Sven feel strange. "You've been in Battle Creek?"

He nodded. "On the farm for almost two months and then three weeks one block from the hospital."

Mrs. Schmidt smiled broadly. "Did you know we have become Seventh-day Adventists?"

"That book!" Sven exclaimed.

Mrs. Schmidt clapped her hands and laughed aloud. "You're right! It was that book. I hope that our new ways don't cause you to change your mind and look for another home just when we have our hearts set on you becoming one of us."

"It will be all right," Sven said, though still feeling strange. Was God trying to turn him into an Adventist? It almost seemed that He was.

* * * * *

At school the following day, Sven stood beside the teacher's desk while she recorded information in her class book.

"Sven Anderson, age thirteen. Birthdate, February twenty-one, eighteen seventy, Oaststad, Sweden."

"Grade?" she asked.

Sven did not know what to answer.

"What level?" she asked.

"I don't know," Sven said. "I haven't been in school since I was eleven."

"Where did you attend school last year?" She seemed not to hear.

Sven felt his spine straightening. He thought of Bobby and Sam working in the forests to the north. He thought of Isaiah and Jamie and Noodge.

"Last year's school?" the teacher asked again.

"I was in the pineries on Pinch River," Sven said proudly.

He had a lot to learn in school, but he'd learned a lot in the year and more since coming to America. He didn't aim to become a doctor or a lawyer. He still aimed to become a farmer, perhaps in the West on the frontier.

Epilogue

He had thought it never would happen, but now it was happening. Sven stood on the railroad platform in Brainerd, Minnesota, listening to the train whistle for the crossing a mile east of town. He took his watch from his pocket. *Eleven-fifty-two. Right on time.* He looked across the street, where his team waited with a two-seater buggy. He looked once at his wife, pleased that she looked so well after her last illness, pleased that she had been well enough to come with him to meet the train, glad the spring day was mild.

"Isn't it wonderful how God has led?" his wife said. "First bringing you into the Advent message in America while He was leading your mother and sister to it in Sweden, and then helping you to find each other after all these years?"

"I may not know Lesja," he worried.

His wife took the photo of his sister from her pocketbook, and they smiled at each other.

The train pulled up at the station, and the brakes hissed along the tracks. The trainman set the step in place beside the passenger coach, and passengers pressed toward the door. Through the window, Sven saw a tall woman in a brown hat waving to him. Behind her, leaning forward to see around a fat man with a large parcel, an old woman peered out.

"It's Mama!" Sven cried, and his wife gripped his arm.

The stream of people came down the steps slowly, wrestling their hand baggage, greeting friends, and blocking the exit. Finally, the two tall women appeared in the doorway. Sven stepped forward to meet them, both hands outstretched. What they had thought at parting would be two years had stretched into nearly eighteen.

"Lesja!" cried Sven Anderson. "Mama!"

The fat man with the parcel saw at once that this was no ordinary meeting. He sprang from the step to make room for the two women.

"Sven!"

If you enjoyed this book,
you should know about these other books by Helen Pyke:

Dr. Walter C. Utt wrote four manuscripts on the French Reformation in story form. Only two of them were published in his lifetime. Helen Godfrey Pyke has now completed and edited the unfinished materials. All parts of the story are now in these two books.

No Peace for a Soldier
Walter C. Utt/Helen Pyke

Part One recognizes the devout French Protestants of the seventeenth century who combined faith and works in heroic proportions. During severe persecutions, while some abandoned their faith, others were martyred. Part One follows a Huguenot family and a family friend from long ago—forced to choose between loyalty to his king or to his God.

Part Two follows the exiles to Holland after the Edict of Revocation eliminated the rights of non-Catholics in France. While many can suffer martyrdom with sufficient heroism, not all are cut out to live their faith through long adversity.
Paperback, 256 pages.
ISBN 13: 978-0-8163-2172-8.   ISBN 10: 0-8163-2172-8.

Any Sacrifice but Conscience
Walter C. Utt/Helen Pyke

Part One chronicles the "Glorious Return" of the Vaudois (Waldenses) to their valleys. Although their soldiers numbered less than a thousand, they fought against the king of France and the duke of Savoy and their 20,000 soldiers. Miraculously, they reenter their lands and reestablish their worship of God which had been forbidden for three and a half years.

Part Two follows the Huguenots who had hastened to join others in exile in assisting them in liberating their brethren on their return to France. They were yet exiles themselves, often hungry or penniless. Would God work a miracle for them?
Paperback, 256 pages.
ISBN 13: 978-0-8163-2171-1.   ISBN 10: 0-8163-2171-X.

Three ways to order:
1. Local Adventist Book Center®
2. Call 1-800-765-6955
3. Shop AdventistBookCenter.com